ANNALISE

Twenty years everlasting...

a novel written by
Myla Athitang

Copyright © 2020 Myla Athitang

All rights reserved

ISBN-13: 978-1-7085-2068-7

ANNALISE

※ 2

Chapter One

❄

Benji

I PATTED THE BACK of a rusty shovel against the soft snow, compressing it into a hard protective shell. Its purity had been corrupted by the dark red mud which laid beneath it. My hands began to numb in the presence of the frigid air. I released my grip on the wooden shaft, allowing the tool to fall by my feet. The shovel, disproportionate to my height, landed in the snow with a muffled thud. In an attempt to return the sensation to my partially frostbitten fingers, I shoved both hands deep into my pockets, which were slightly damp from my previous attempts to do so. To no avail, I pulled them back out and rubbed them together. Gradually, I began to feel my fingertips again. I slid my hands back and forth rapidly—then stopped. The numbness immediately returned.

The tree limbs rustled in a soothing manner, and small specks of white dust descended from their branches. I reached back into my right pocket and pulled out a moist, crumpled piece of notebook paper, unraveling it and placing it gently on top of the beaten snow. The bleeding ink coalesced into a single blob of blue. The once present words were no longer legible.

I exhaled sharply, seeing my breath form as a mist in front of my eyes. The corners of my lips curled upward. I quickly inhaled and exhaled again, creating a larger cloud of condensation. It reminded me of the dragons who protected the princesses in all the fairytales my mother read to me. It sounded silly now, but this perceived creature had the most captivating features, and I almost felt sorry for it. I continued impersonating the creature, giggling between breaths. I did so until I began to feel lightheaded. A heavy weight developed in my chest along with a tingling sensation forming behind the bridge of my nose.

I slumped down onto my knees with my hands buried deeply in the snow. Small voids began to appear in the pillow of white beneath me. I peered upward, searching for the source. With the suspicion of dripping tree branches and leaves, I looked downward again, catching a glimpse of the glistening drop falling from my chin and dissolving into the snow. My cheeks had numbed to the point I couldn't feel the tears leaking from my eyes. I clutched the rim of my sleeve and moved it toward my face. In an attempt to dry my tears, I swiped the sleeve across my eyes. The burning sensation behind my nose intensified as I wiped with my sleeves over and over again. My lips quivered. I threw my arms across my chest in frustration, clutching my shoulders, and leaned toward the ground.

"It's okay, Clyde. You'll be okay..." I cooed softly.

As I recited it repeatedly to myself, I rocked vigorously in a sullen state. *Inhale. Exhale.* Again, *Inhale. Exhale.* I shook my head. My face felt warm. A tear rolled down my cheek, and I felt it this time. *Inhale. Exhale.* Again, *Inhale. Exhale.* The quivering became apparent in every breath I took. The next breath escaped with a soft whimper.

"It's okay, Clyde. Don't cry. Benji is okay..." I repeated.

The words I heavily depended on had lost their meaning by now. The barking of neighborhood dogs echoed throughout the woods. I tightened my embrace, now clutching the fabric on my shoulders until my fingers turned white. One last bark erupted from a neighborhood dog, sending me into cascading tears. I completely collapsed, still sobbing into my sleeves. My throat seemed to partially close off, inducing me to inhale sharply. I felt the iciness collecting in my lungs. A shiver ran down my spine. The intervals between breaths became shorter, and I completely lost all my focus.

The woolen fibers scratched my skin as I tore the leaden scarf from my neck. A breeze swept by, swiftly whipping the fringes at the end of my scarf into a frenzy. I neatly placed it upon the beaten snow and tucked the crumpled paper between the folds so it wouldn't blow away. While still situated on the damp ground, I loaded the blanket-covered wagon with the large shovel. Finally, I rose up on my feet, pausing for a second to assure warmth to my long-buried friend, and trudged onward toward my home nestled on the outskirts of the city with the wagon trailing behind me.

Someone once told me a candlelight could be seen miles away as long as the weather and air condition permitted it. On the edge of my windowsill sat a vanilla-scented candle. I used it to guide me back home most nights; however, being twilight, I depended on my memory to get me home. My mother lit the candle every morning, blew it out after lunch, relit it for dinner, and laid it to rest before I went to sleep. She believed it brought positive karma to the household and ensured my safety. At the time, I couldn't grasp the concept of faith in an undefinable object. I had never met another soul who relied on something so desperately, but I'm confident every living creature on this planet would have coveted her happiness and wellbeing as much as she did.

The white fluff frozen to the base of my shoe melted into the asphalt, slickening the road as I walked. The narrow distance to the town became haunted with solitude. I imagined a wicked witch named Greta Grindel who put a curse on this part of the town. It was my only explanation for the feeling of emptiness at the time. The trees were bare alongside the road, collecting clumps of white on their delicate branches. Peeking through the clouds hid a timid sun, speckling light onto the town. The snow showers persisted day and night. My mother would often christen the weather "impolite" for interrupting the sunlight cast upon the earth. However, I do understand the contrary. The sun can be overwhelming at times with blistering heat bludgeoning us in heaving waves. Furthermore, it emits harmful rays in spite of those who disregard the application of sunscreen—or so I've been told.

An empty paper bag skidded across the asphalt, being slung into the air with a gust of wind coming from behind me. It blew toward the mighty clock hovering over the miniature town of Caershire, Pennsylvania. Caershire was a little town back in the day. It was small but comfy. I had everything I needed back then. The arcade was situated between *Out of the Bleu Bakery* and *Shaggy's Music Shack.* My father's property in the woods was only a five-minute walk from my home on heavy snowfall days and a one-minute walk on clear days. I was also homeschooled, so I was home most of the time. Being in Caershire drew this connection that I hadn't felt anywhere else.

"Clyde!" I heard my mother call from the front porch.

Her silhouette became clearer the closer to her I got. Eventually, I was able to see the edges of her lips curled downward in a frown. In her hands were a pink quilt and a freshly washed red-striped towel. She opened her arms wide to me, an invitation I couldn't turn down. Without hesitation, she embraced me in her arms, her body radiating with warmth and acceptance.

"Don't you ever leave without telling me, again! I was worried sick!" Mother rebuked. "Come inside. It's cold out there."

She hastily draped the towel over my jacket and then wrapped me tightly in the quilt, clutching the excess fabric behind me as I walked inside. Immediately, the aroma of baked rosemary and chicken burst into the air. I quickly removed my shoes and stacked them on the shelf above my nametag.

"I made your favorite, mashed potatoes, and I added a little bit of the sharp cheddar cheese your father picked up from the store. Smells good, doesn't it?" She flashed a smile.

I nodded, slightly distracted by the hidden scent of baked banana bread.

"Ah, I knew I couldn't trick that little nose of yours," she added, proceeding to lightly tap the tip of my reddened nose.

I crinkled my face, giggling childishly. Her magic touches seemed to brighten the mood immediately. My mother had a heart of gold. She grew up here in Caershire and never looked away from the small town. She'd feel too guilty if she did.

"Go wash up before dinner. There should be some warm water left over from this morning." Her hands ran through my hair after removing my hat. "Remember to save some water for Daddy, okay?"

"Don't eat without me, please," I said, raising my tiny pinkie. "Promise me."

She chuckled, intertwining hers with mine. "I promise."

I shed the hefty layers of wool and linen and charged up to the bathroom. Neatly folded towels along with a few toiletries rested on the counter. The reflective countertops and checkered curtains gave the bathroom a distinctive character. For some odd reason, this was my favorite room in the entire house. As entertainment, I hid toys and crackers in small compartments and crevices in the bathroom, naively anticipating a cleaning fairy would pick them up. Little did I know that Mother was the fairy the whole time.

I rotated the handle above the faucet until the arrow pointed toward the red tape plastered over the right side of the black and white-tiled wall. A stream of icy-cold water shot out of the faucet opening, choking up slightly, then ceased the flow of water entirely. I hopped into the tub, kicking aside all my toys, and crouched down on all fours to peer under the faucet opening. A droplet of water landed on my forehead. I pulled away, wiping at the cold wet spot. Puzzled, I rotated the handle back to its original position and stepped out of the tub. As I left the bathroom to get help from my mother, I noticed something at the end of the hallway, a red rubber ball marked in black sharpie, "Benji". The sudden jingling of bells raised the anticipation of seeing my best friend, hoping to watch him scamper out of my room and into my arms, but that was not the case. The sound of bells echoed from the back door entrance of the kitchen. I continued making my way quickly down the steps.

Upon entering the kitchen, I caught my mother in the midst of her evening cleaning. Mesmerized by this process, I stood idly by, patiently waiting for an opportunity to ask for her help without interrupting her ritual. She rummaged through the chaotic cupboard of spices and seasonings while wearing her bright yellow rubber gloves, setting aside coriander and pepper. Reaching further in, she pulled out an aluminum coffee container. In her first attempt to unscrew the lid, the rubber gloves made it almost impossible for her to accomplish. She pacely pulled off the glove from her right hand, finger by finger, then unscrewed the lid with ease. I wasn't able to see inside the old coffee can, but I had no reason to believe it contained anything other than coffee grounds. With her sitting on the floor peering into the container, I found this to be the perfect opportunity to finally make my presence known.

"Mother, the bath is broken," I blurted out.

My words seemed to have startled my mother. Her hand clutched her chest in sudden shock.

"I'll take a look at the spigot. Go change out of your clothes, Sweetie." She placed the open container on the counter along with the coriander and pepper.

I stepped inside the kitchen, allowing for some room through the narrow door frame. The rickety old stairs creaked as my mother marched up to the bathroom. A single candle illuminated the kitchen along with the help of some patches of sunlight peeking through the cracks of the blinds covered with years of neglect. My mother liked it when the kitchen was dim. You couldn't see the dust nor the spider webs forming on the taller shelves where she couldn't reach.

The clock situated above the kitchen window ticked endlessly. *Tick. Tock. Tick. Tock.* Six o'clock. My father's schedule ended around 7:00. It gave Mother an ample amount of time to set the table for dinner and relax for a bit afterwards. Her favorite pastimes, other than cleaning, were reading and gardening. Unfortunately, the weather had made it almost impossible for gardening, so she had her nose deep in *The Giver*. The book laid face open on the kitchen table with a bright yellow piece of paper jammed in the gutter. The pages would flap ever so often from gentle breezes provided by the kitchen fan, which dispersed the cooking smoke and delicious aromas throughout the entire house.

"Clyde, the water is working now," my mother informed me while she was returning down the steps.

As she reached the last step, her dress caught beneath her feet, and she stumbled down the bottom step to the floor. She quickly recovered, holding onto the railing for support, and continued toward the kitchen, acting as if the incident never occurred.

When her slightly ashamed gaze caught mine, she narrowed her eyes.

"I told you to go change, didn't I? You're going to get awfully sick in those clothes." Her hands were tightly posed on her hips.

I just stood there in silence, twiddling my thumbs.

"Well? Aren't you going up?" Mother's fingers tapped against her slim waist.

I remember feeling vividly a pair of hands came up from the floor, restraining my feet in a locked position. In my head, I was telling them to move, but they weren't compliant in any way. The feeling ascended my entire legs to my torso. In my stomach, hunger and fullness coexisted, battling each other to become the dominant discomfort. A loud grumble erupted from my gut, blocking out every thought racing through my mind. Could my mother hear it? Would she have known? It inched its way up to my chest. I could feel and hear the blood pulsing through my veins. The discomfort reached my throat, almost closing it off entirely. Finally, it devoured my entire head in one gigantic gulp. Now, another feeling surfaced. This time, it arose from my esophagus to the tip of my tongue.

"May I ask you something?" I queried abruptly.

Her face tensed in concern .

"What's wrong?" Mother relaxed her arms, letting them fall by her waist freely.

After my rude injection, sudden dryness in my mouth became apparent.

"Um...Benji..." My gaze shifted down to the floor, alternating the pressure from the pads of my feet to my heels "...he'll be okay, won't he?"

My mother's lack of words caused me to lift my head as I anticipated a reply. Her gaze locked onto mine.

"Benji–" she paused "–Benji will be okay, Sweetheart. I'm sure he appreciates what you have been doing for him his entire life."

My mother crouched down in front of me, placing her toasty hands on my shoulders. Her mouth opened, as if she wanted to say something, but she decided to embrace me instead.

The headlights of a passing car lit up the room for a mere second.

"Benji loved you very much, Clyde. I'm sure of it. He loved you just as much as Mommy and Daddy love you." She pulled away and gave me a peck on the forehead. "He was just sick. That wasn't your fault."

I shielded my eyes from her view, but a mother's intuition had a reputation for being extraordinarily strong.

"It's okay, Clyde."

I fell into her arms once more, sobbing on her shoulder, as she wrapped both arms around me.

"Sometimes, things just happen. We don't know why or how or what causes them. It just happens. We have no choice but to accept them and keep moving on with our lives." Mother closed her hands around mine, holding them up to her chin. "You just have to find the strength to move on, not only for you, but for Benji. Okay?"

I wiped away a tear and nodded, "O...O-kay."

"Let's go get you bathed and ready for dinner. Daddy will be home soon."

Mother's hand rested against the flat of my back, ever so slightly urging me forward. I held on to the wooden railing, gliding my hand over the surface as I reached the each step. I sniffled as she ushered me into the bathroom. The bathtub was filled a few inches high with warm soapy water. My toys floated about mindlessly, occasionally bumping into each other—then parting ways. Clumped up around the rim of the tub were clouds of bubbling foam. A few rubber ducks fell victim to these floating obstacles, completely being devoured by the suds. My mother discreetly shut the door behind her as she returned to her duties. After a momentary lapse in reality, I took this as a sign that I needed to snap back into the way I usually functioned every day, pretending that Benji never died and I never lost my best friend.

I promptly undressed, dropping my clothes in the hamper by the door haphazardly. In spite of the fact that it had been quite awhile since the faucet had been turned on, the water remained lukewarm, as if it was waiting for me to appear. As I dropped into the deep tub, the ducks and boats seemed to scurry away. It was only after the walls of the tub became an obstacle for their escape. After ricocheting back toward my direction, they came begging to befriend me again.

"I didn't want to play with you anyways," I thought to myself.

The nose of Marvin, one exceptionally mischievous duck, tapped against my knee, staring up at me with his glossy black eyes. The sailboat came next and then the rocketship. I hesitated giving in at first, but they were tempting.

"Pick me up!" Marvin demanded

"Help me steer the boat," said the tiny sailor in the bright yellow sailboat.

The rocketship never spoke.

Temptations overcame me as I scooped up the duck, balancing it on the edge of the tub, then releasing it to slide down into the sudsy water. The splash sent a frenzy of bubbles into the air, some of them finding their way out of the tub. Soaring upward, the rocketship created an ear-splitting **BOOM!** –then plunged into the depths of the oceanic bath. Waves formed from the crash, flipping over the sailboat with a vigorous tumble. The sailor, whose body hung halfway out of the side window, struggled to regain control of the sailboat. With a graceful motion, I set the vehicle upright, gently sliding my hand against the hull. The sailor waved in my direction as a thank you for the rescue.

A tense vibe came from behind. As I turned around, I noticed the familiar color of yellow reflecting off of the porcelain bathtub. A whole army of ducks with Marvin as their leader commanded my attention. I steered their path toward the faucet by creating a current with my hand. One by one, the ducks followed Marvin in a singular formation. I cupped a handful of water, showering each of the ducks lightly. The stream of water, bearing considerable weight on the smaller ducks, caused them to stray from the original lineup. Marvin spun around in disapproval. His beady eyes seemed to narrow for a split second.

An immediate feeling of guilt overcame me. I reached into the water and yanked out the plug, creating a funnel into the drain. Out of the corner of my eye, I spotted a dry bar of Cerulean blue soap sitting in a small porcelain dish on the edge of the tub. As the last bit of bathwater spiraled into the darkness, I grabbed the bar of soap and soaked it generously then placed it back into the dish.

I heard the sound of ringing bells coming from beyond the bathroom door. The thumping of bulky boots resonating from the ground floor signaled my father's return home. The clanking of cheap china plates enticed me along with the trailing aroma of freshly baked chicken. I hopped out of the tub and wrapped a worn-out towel around myself. As I shuffled toward my room, I noticed the silhouette of my father and mother standing close together. No words were being said. My mother just nodded then pressed her head into my father's chest. His hand rested against her upper back then shifted downward to her lower back. He gently kissed the top of her head, pulling her closer to his side.

I scurried into my room, spotting a neatly folded outfit laid on my bed, a pair of chino pants with an oversized, slightly stained ThunderCats T-shirt. I changed into my clean clothes, tying off the excess fabric from my T-shirt with a rubber band.

"Clyde, hurry down for dinner! The food will get cold!" My mother shouted from the kitchen.

I stuffed the towel into the overflowing hamper and raced out the door.

My father and mother sat across from each other. I picked up on another peculiar feeling. The atmosphere was tense. A dollop of mashed potatoes accompanied with a slab of baked chicken sat solemnly in the center of their plates. My mother began picking at her food with the tip of her fork, sliding away pieces of burnt chicken. I crept up behind my father and poked my head into his peripheral vision. He faced me, a smile widening on his face.

"Hey, Buddy." He tussled my hair with his calloused hands. "Didn't you just take a bath? Why is your hair so dry?"

He side-eyed my mother slightly, but she seemed unbothered.

I sat on my side of the table. My plate overflowed with creamy mashed potatoes filled with yellow strips of cheddar and a colossal chunk of chicken. A glass of cold milk sat on a small square napkin behind the plate. Immediately, I scooped up a glob of mashed potatoes and topped it with a piece of chicken, but before I could eat it, my mother abruptly set her utensils down on the table.

"Clyde–" she pursed her lips "–do you know what day it is?"

I glanced over to the calendar hanging above the key holders.

"It's…" I narrowed my eyes and with little confidence said "…Tuesday?"

"Well, yes. What else?" Mother seemed slightly amused.

I considered the question, eventually shrugging my shoulders as if I was unsure of the answer.

Mother revealed a sapphire-colored velvet box hidden underneath a checkered cloth.

"Happy Eighth Birthday," she stated.

I sat in silence, idiotically. I looked over to my father to which he nodded in approval. His eyebrows furrowed slightly as his smile twitched.

My mother gently slid the box over to my side of the table. I graciously accepted the present. I stared in awe at the sheen of the blue velvet. It had the texture of tiny soft bristles, gliding against the tips of my fingers. The smell was of fresh cedar wood. I took my sleeve and rubbed it against the surface. The sound gave me goosebumps. It was soothing, I would say.

Marking another milestone in my life, this was the first time I had held or even seen velvet. It was a rarity around town. A few kids around my age would gossip about some of their out-of-town friends receiving velvet coats and hats for Christmas. No one in Caershire, Pennsylvania owned velvet coats.

I could hear my green army men and small dice call from the bedroom. They seemed to have sensed the box's presence. It made me wonder what I could do with this present. The size was a bit too small to fit my Power Rangers action figure or my shiny rocketship. However, my smaller toys would fit perfectly inside the box as a hideout during battles.

A couple of angry squeaks emitted from the bathroom. Marvin must have sensed it, also. He could get jealous and very possessive at times.

"Floating dry land for my young ducklings!" shouted Marvin.

I wasn't sure if the box could float. It seemed pretty heavy, and I wouldn't want to ruin the velvet.

I couldn't express my gratitude for the present enough. I hopped off my seat and gave my mother a hug and then walked over to my father. His hands reached under my arms, and he lifted me up into the air. The once chillingly silent room was now filled with warmth and laughter. He set me into my chair and fell back into his. Although I was extremely grateful for the present, I was starving! Without any hesitation, I dug into the mashed potatoes again with the spoon and stuffed the whole thing into my mouth.

My mother shook her head.

"I'm flattered," she chuckled. "You must really like my cooking. You haven't even opened your present, and you're eating like an absolute horse."

I momentarily paused from chewing at the realization that the velvet box itself wasn't the present. I left my fork on the plate, letting it sink into the mash then pulled the box closer to me. It had a golden latch with a tiny embroidered rose in the top right corner of the lid. I snapped the latch upward and lifted the top. A familiar device awaited its discovery. The box held a medium sized cube composed of colorful blocks.

I took it out of the box, resting it on the palm of my hand. Occasionally, I would lift it up to inspect the device.

"Does he even know what it is?" My father muttered to my mother with his hand hiding his mouth.

My mother's face went blank for a second. She cleared her throat, turning toward me.

"Well–" she paused "–do you like it?"

A few kids had their hands busy with this device near the playground. I remember them twisting and turning the numerous rows, but I couldn't understand what they were trying to achieve.

"It's neat…" I kept my gaze on the brightly colored array of squares.

"Let me show you something…"

My father lifted the cube from my hands, holding it in place between his index finger and thumb.

"This is called a Rubik's Cube. It's a… puzzle, of sorts." He leaned in closer. "The end goal is to try and match the colors on one side of the cube, like this…"

He rotated the top row a couple of times, settling on a top row: GREEN, WHITE, GREEN. He took the center, twisting it downward a couple of times. There were no other green blocks on that middle column.

"Oh–well… you'd probably figure this out better than I could." He placed the cube back in the lush velvet box.

I shut the lid and closed the latch.

"Can I take this to my room?" I asked.

"Of course. Make sure you come back down to finish your food," my mother replied.

I hopped out of my seat, clutching the velvet box with both hands. I sped up the stairs to my room. Conveniently, a section of my nightstand remained bare. I gently set down the box, aligning the corner with the edges of the nightstand.

A reddish cast fell upon the room as the bright sun laid away to rest. The golden rays glazed over the pure white snow covering our front lawn. I pressed the palm of my hand against the slightly-cracked glass window. Somewhere out in the woods, Benji waited. He was patient and never spoke out of line nor made a ruckus. He was a good dog, a great one.

"Clyde." The door gently swung open with my father standing behind it. "Your mother just told me you left to go out into the woods by yourself. Is it true? You went out by yourself?"

"I just went to visit Benji. I gave him a toy," I replied.

A glaze fell over his eyes. He crouched down in front of me.

"I know you miss him, but… mommy and I can't afford to lose you too. I need you to promise me you'll be here to protect your mother, okay?" He cupped his hands around mine.

"Can you take me to see him tomorrow…?" I asked, hopeful for a positive reply.

His eyes moved downward as he sighed.

24

"Okay."

Chapter Two

❄

My Name

THE SMELLS OF BLUEBERRY pancakes and bacon along with rattle of blinds woke me from my slumber. My eyes stung as I introduced them to the sunlight. My mother stood at the foot of my bed, folding my clothes and placing them into the drawers.

"Good morning," she softly spoke when she saw my eyes flicker open.

"Morning..." I croaked, not as softly and daintily.

I sat upright, contemplating going back to sleep. The clock read six o'clock in the morning, my mother's peak hour.

"Come along. Your hair is all knotted from sleep."

She escorted me to the bathroom, setting aside a fresh towel before turning on the sink water. Dousing her fingertips ever so slightly with icy water, she combed through my hair. Once in awhile, her fingers would get caught in the tiny knots, making me flinch.

"I left your toothbrush in the cup. Brush your teeth while I comb your hair, please."

I did as told, reaching over to pick up the toothbrush. I felt slightly restrained by my mother's hands, but I managed to snatch the toothbrush out of the cup. I smeared a bit of toothpaste onto the bristles and wet the brush under the running faucet.

"Remember to get behind the teeth. The tooth fairy wouldn't appreciate another cavity," Mom said while working on another troublesome knot.

I quickly brushed my teeth in hopes of speeding up the entire morning process.

"Where is Dad?" I asked, my words barely understandable with the toothbrush hanging halfway out of my mouth.

"He's downstairs shining his shoes. Why?"

"He's taking me to see Benji." I spat into the tap, flushing it with cold water then rinsed my mouth.

My mom stopped brushing my hair. Her hands rested on my shoulders.

"I have to run downstairs. Your clothes are on the dresser, okay?" She patted me on the back as she left the room.

I nodded.

My mother then swiftly exited the bathroom, going down the steps in a hasty manner. Fortunately, I found this to be the perfect opportunity to hide my toys in the bathroom. I ran to my room, lifting up the lid of my toy chest. A few army men were scattered along the bottom of the chest. I gathered around two or three of them and then hurried back to the bathroom. My favorite hiding spots were in the soap dish, behind the toilet, and under the folded towels. Since I was in a hurry, I stuck the toys in the same places I normally hid them in. Usually, I would switch up my hiding places, but since I had plans that day, I did a fairly amateur job.

After I was done hiding my toys for the cleaning fairy, I headed back to my room to get dressed. Passing by the top of the staircase, I heard whispers from my mother and father. My mother rambled quiet nonsense while my father interjected a few mumbles of "mm-hmm" and "okay". I continued to my room, spotting the neatly folded outfit resting upon my dresser. Mother picked out a worn-out T-shirt with denim jeans and my father's old coat on the side. I slipped on the T-shirt and jeans then wrapped myself loosely in the large coat.

The window, covered with frost, made it hard to see through. I took my sleeve and swiped it across the screen to reveal the view of the woods. Soon. I'd be there soon.

"Clyde, you ready?" My father's head peeked through the door opening.

I nodded and trotted out of the room.

Before leaving the house, I waved goodbye to my mother, who was shining the glass cups with a soft cloth.

Father decided to pull me to the woods on my wagon since the car had some trouble starting that morning. My father had just entered into the peak of his "old man years" as he called it. He'd curse his knee pains and blamed his age, but his knees were always bad, which allowed for him to drive his precious truck as much as possible.

I laid on a blanket that I brought to make the ride a comfortable one. The sun hadn't broken through the grayish clouds, allowing me to gaze up and wonder about nothing in particular without a single care. I began to imagine the conversations I was going to have with Benji. I wanted to ask him if he missed being home or if he was hungry. Unfortunately, I forgot to bring him treats. He loved the biscuits Mother picked up from the grocery store. I should have brought him a biscuit or two. Maybe his favorite red ball would have been appropriate, too. He loved that red ball.

"Are you okay back there?" Father asked, pulling aside to take a short break.

He kicked out his leg, in and out again, and rubbed his aching knees.

"Yes," I replied, peering up at the sky.

"What are you so focused on?" His eyes traced the path of mine. "The clouds? They're pretty, huh?"

"How come I can't touch them?" I reached up as high as I could, attempting to grab the floating bundles of cotton.

It always felt like they were sifting through my fingers, but I could never quite reach them.

"You've always been a big dreamer," Dad chuckled.

After the short break, we continued on our journey. I flipped over, looking down at the asphalt as the wagon rode along on top of it. My father's footprints had left large imprints leading back to the house along with tire tracks from passing cars.

I laid my head against my folded arms. It felt comfortable in this position. The world finally felt at peace. I closed my eyes, picturing Benji's wagging tail and soft paws. Soon, I would be reunited with my best friend.

"Clyde, we're here."

❋ 30

I opened my eyes, squinting as the purely white snow reflected the sunlight from above. My father waited patiently for me to get out of the wagon. I swung my legs over the side. My father lifted me off, gently placing me down on the ground. He held my hand as I guided him to the spot. Before we made it far into the woods, Dad's cell phone began to ring inconsiderately. The color drained from his face. There was a look of guilt that pulled the front of his brows upward as if to say *sorry*. His hand released mine as he went to retrieve his phone.

"I, um, need... I need to make a phone call. Come on. I'll be quick." He reached to grab my hand again.

I stepped back. I didn't want to leave knowing that within these woods, Benji awaited for my arrival.

Dad let out a sigh and nodded.

"Okay, just stay here. I'll be right back," he said then ran off.

He shouted a few more directions, but I tuned out everything after he fled. He'd been fighting for a new job for months. Calls after calls and interviews after interviews, he remained as a steelworker for some steel mill on the outskirts of town. It was a rough job. His hands were full of calluses and scars. They weren't soft like Mother's.

I turned my back and walked away. To find my way to Benji, I used a simple trick to remember. The grave was 27 steps in the direction of where the arrow engraved on the dogwood tree was pointing. I placed my back against the tree then began stepping one foot in front of the other, counting as I walked. Step after step, I counted until I reached 27. My wool scarf rested on top of the burial site where I had left it. I dropped to my knees, ready to spill my thoughts.

I opened my mouth to speak, but my throat closed up.

"Come on. Say something," I thought to myself.

I attempted to speak once more. Not a word left my mouth.

My hopefulness transformed right in front of me in a taunting manner. The small breezes began to pick up speed, sweeping up the snow into a giant blinding mass. The trees danced angrily to the wailing cries of the wind. It was deafening but quiet at the same time.

Frustrated, I pulled the hood of my father's coat over my head. The coat was big enough to swallow me whole. I tightened my grip on the sleeves like my life depended on it. I closed my eyes and tried to imagine Benji. I tried to feel his soft fur brushing up against me. I tried to recreate the happiness from receiving the ball after he fetched it. I wanted to relive the moment when I first laid my eyes on him at the adoption center. I tried to revive him. I really tried.

※ 32

Muffled footsteps sounded in the distance. Light, feather-like steps. Sounds a large man couldn't have made. I didn't sense danger nor a threat, so my eyes remained closed.

Was it Benji?

No. Benji's gone.

Was it my father?

No. The footsteps seemed too light.

To whom did these footsteps belong to?

"What's his name?" A high-pitched voice asked.

I opened my eyes, pulling the hood off my head. The silhouette of a small figure stood before me. It soon cleared into a visible view of the girl who was around the same age as I was, standing in front of me with her hands held behind her back. Her skin, pale as porcelain, almost blended with the snow. As the clouds parted, a bit of sunlight shined her way, making her blue eyes sparkle. Her cheeks were rosy pink with a few freckles appearing on her nose and some on her cheeks. Her lips were glossed over with red tint. Truly angelic.

"His name?" she repeated.

"His... His name? His name is Benji." I continued gazing up at the girl.

She knelt down, joining me on the ground.

"Well, what happened to him?"

"He got sick and passed away. Mother says he's up in Doggy Heaven now." I pointed toward the sky.

She peered upward.

"Doggy Heaven… such a place, eh?" She smiled, confidently displaying her pearly white teeth. "Wouldn't it be nice to visit Doggy Heaven?"

I nodded vigorously.

"My mother said Benji is watching me from above. I wanted to say something to him, but I got nervous…"

"Well, you still can." She straightened her posture then peered up toward the sky. "Excuse me, Benji. Hello- Hi! Um… this might seem strange, but… we are here today to speak with you and see how you are doing in Doggy Heaven."

She shot a quick glance at me, signaling for my turn to speak.

I attempted to say something but held my tongue.

"Psst… it's your turn," she whispered.

"I… I don't know what to say…"

As her eager face fell into disappointment, I had a sudden instinct to flee. Maybe it was because I felt embarrassed from not being able to communicate with my best friend while a complete stranger could do it without a second thought. For her, it was effortless. How come I struggled so much?

Her hands wrapped around mine. "Whenever you're ready, okay?"

I guess she felt that I wanted to run away. She held my hands tightly.

"Okay." I took a deep breath in. "Benji... hi. How- How are you? Are you... doing good up there?"

I eyed the girl.

Her face went blank for a second.

Suddenly, her eyes widened. "Oh! I hear him!"

"You do?" I queried.

She bobbed her head. "He says he's doing great! And, and... that he misses you! Yes! He misses you very much!"

I broadened my smile, marveling over her abilities to communicate with Benji. However, I still felt slightly jealous at the same time because I couldn't hear him and the girl could. She seemed to get an answer immediately, and all I got was a couple of barks from the neighborhood dogs.

"Okay, um... next question: when can I come visit you?" I asked anxiously.

She paused for a second. Her eyes shifted to the ground in a sudden focus.

"Um..." she mumbled.

I was on the edge of my seat. I was usually patient, but I couldn't wait to hear what Benji had to say.

"Well?" I pried.

Her pointer finger raised as if to say *wait*. She went back into full concentration.

I played with the cuffs of my father's coat. A car passed by in the distance, running over a few twigs on the road.

"He says soon! Very soon!" She giddily said.

Suddenly, a whole range of questions came to my mind. Before I could ask another, the girl opened her mouth to speak again.

"Hey, how come your eyes are red and puffy? Are you allergic to something?" Her head tilted slightly.

"My eyes?" The question caught me somewhat off guard.

"No. You were crying, weren't you?" She inched closer.

Was I? Had I become that numb to my own emotions?

She reached into her side pockets and slipped on a pair of bright yellow mittens, placing them against my cheeks soon after. I pulled away, but she was persistent.

"Stay still, will ya?" She pressed harder. "There... are you warm now?"

I placed my hands on top of hers. "Yes..."

My eyes fell upon the name, ANNALISE A. LYNN, embroidered on her upper coat pocket in white thread.

"Anna- Annalise?" I stuttered.

She looked down at her pocket. "Yep, that's my name. And you are... *Tom*?"

※ 36

I raised my eyebrow to the name that wasn't mine. I peered down at my breast pocket, realizing that this was my father's coat, and I shook my head.

"This isn't my–"

"Son!" my father called from afar.

Annalise seemed to panic, hopping up on her feet.

"It was nice meeting you, Tom, but I really have to go now." She turned away, trudging against the strong wind.

"Wait! I'm not–" I watched as she soon became fully engulfed in the flurry of snow "–Tom…"

Hands appeared out of nowhere, snatching my right arm. I let out a yelp as the suddenness startled me.

"Clyde, quiet down! The snow storm is coming this way. We have to go, now." Father lifted me up into his arms, carrying me out of the woods.

The wagon, tilted over on its side, had begun to accumulate snow. My blanket laid on the ground, now soaking wet.

"C'mon, get in." He lifted the wagon back upright and placed me in it.

The blanket was rolled up and tucked in the small space in front of me. The handle of the wagon lifted, and with a short, sharp tug, the wheels began to move out of the snow piles.

"What about Benji?" I asked.

"Benji's resting at the moment. He'll be okay."

Dad's walking pace began to speed up, so I held onto the sides of the wagon tightly.

"The signal out here wasn't the greatest, but luckily the manager was busy. They said to call back 15 minutes after the last attempt. If I make it on time, I could possibly get the warehouse packing job in New Jersey." He lifted his wrist to check the time. "Seven minutes, alright."

The wagon seemed to lose some of its traction against the icy parts of the road, sliding in certain places.

"Can you slow down?" I shouted.

"This wind is no joke. At this rate, I won't have even a second to spare," he continued, completely ignoring my request.

I squeezed the sides of the wagon until my fingers numbed. Each time my father checked his watch, he sped up. Eventually, he began sprinting as the second hand ticked by.

The closer we got, the view of our house became clearer. My mother stood on the porch, frantically waving her hands. Once we reached the driveway, my father released the handle, letting it drop onto the concrete in a sharp *crack*. The wagon eventually came to a stop as it approached the snow clumps barricading the edges of the driveway. My mother helped me out of the wagon then rushed me inside where the fireplace crackled with gentle flames.

"Your father will be on a call, so I need you to be quiet, okay?" Mom removed my coat and boots.

"Is dad really going to New Jersey?" I asked.

"You don't need to worry about that now. Your schoolwork is on your desk. I suggest that you dry off and finish your work before lunchtime."

After my coat was placed on the rack and my shoes were shoved in their cubby, I ran up the stairs to my room. A pile of books sat on my desk along with papers and notebooks galore. However, I wasn't interested in schoolwork.

I opened up a notebook and flipped to an empty page. I pinched the paper near the perforated lines and held down the notebook with my other hand. Slowly, I tore the notebook paper from its bindings, meticulously moving my finger placement as I went down the page to prevent any accidental rips. I laid the paper on top of the closed notebook and then grabbed a red pen, scribbling "*Dear Annalise*" on the top line.

I tapped the tip of the pen on the paper, speckling it with tiny dots. I wasn't completely sure of what else to say. I just met the girl, so I didn't exactly have the intention of spilling my feelings.

Dear Annalise,

Thank you for making me happy today. I think you are very sweet and pretty.

I hope I can see you again and we can talk to Benji another time.

From,
Clyde Whittaker
P.S. My name is not Tom. My father's name is Tom.

I folded the piece of paper and stuck it inside a larger folded piece of colored paper then sealed it off with clear tape. Now, it was ready to be sent.

I raced down the steps and into the living room. My father paced the floor, waiting for the phone call to go through. My mother sat in kitchen, reading *The Giver*.

I laced my boots and slipped on my coat then proceeded out the front door. The mailbox was at the end of the driveway. I wasn't sure what to do after the letter was placed inside. I'd seen my parents flipping up the red flag a couple of times, so I assumed that was what I should do. After placing the letter inside the mailbox, I lifted the red flag and shut the lid. My father popped outside, motioning me to come back in the house. I shifted away from the mailbox, making my way back to the front door.

"Hurry back inside, Boy! It's cold out there!" He shouted, clearly irritated with me.

I trotted inside, removing my coat and my boots.

"Are you out of your mind? It's in the negatives out there, I'm sure. Dear Lord, you've been out one too many times. You're going to get sick now," my mother fussed.

She snatched the coat from me, throwing it up on the hanger.

"Go fetch your homework and come back downstairs. We have the fire going. I don't want you to be cold up there." She dusted my boots on the doormat.

I stood idly by, rocking back and forth on my heels.

Mom clicked her tongue, sharply pointing upward.

"When does the mailman get here?" I asked, completely ignoring her request.

"That's not any of your concern at the moment. Now, go get your homework and come back down."

I marched up the stairs in a petty manner. An overwhelming feeling of anxiety overcame me. I had never been so impatient in my life.

The stack of papers laid untouched on my wooden desk. I grabbed a few worksheet books from different subjects then returned downstairs where my mother and father awaited. A steaming cup of hot cocoa was placed upon the coffee table with the TV turned on and set to a home decor channel. It was my mother who was watching TV. *The Giver* was turned upside down on top of the kitchen table.

"What subject would you like to start with first?" My mother asked. "I suggest starting with English."

She moved the pillows aside, allowing me to sit beside her. I placed my schoolwork down on the table and opened up an easy-to-follow English workbook. There were a few sentences printed on the page with blank lines underneath, which I was instructed to fill in.

"Adrian spotted a fluffy white rabbit in the woods." Her finger traced the first sentence as she read.

"What did Adrian spot in the woods?" I read the first question aloud.

I took my freshly sharpened Ticonderoga pencil and wrote in block letters the word Rabbit.

"Don't be afraid to add to it. What color is it?"

I reread the sentence.

"It was a white rabbit." I assumed she wanted me to add a bit more. "He was fluffy too."

Mother's lips curled into a smile that smoothed out every wrinkle that ever existed upon her cheeks.

"Read the next few lines and answer the questions. I'll be right back." She got up to leave, shuffling into the kitchen.

I did as told, continuing on in the story. To paraphrase, the rabbit gave Adrian a bouncy ball he found in the park. He told Adrian that the bouncy ball was very special. I couldn't quite understand why that ball was so special. It was a regular ball, round, bouncy, green, and small. There wasn't any major significance details in the text. It was just a regular green bouncy ball.

Out of all of my toys, the bouncy ball was the most basic. I couldn't figure out why exactly. I just couldn't find excitement in bouncing something up and down. In fact, it was a headache just keeping up with it. Along with this, it didn't bounce to an incredible height. I believe it touched the ceiling at one point, but that was long ago. I tried to imagine the different ways a bouncy ball could be special. If it lit up in the night sky like a star, it would be special. If it bounced 100 feet into the air, it would be special. However, it was just a regular bouncy ball.

"How far have you gotten?" My mother entered the living room with a plateful of cookies. "Have you not answered any since I left?"

I looked down at my paper. The lines under the sentences were blank.

"Can I ask you something?"

Mom set the plate of cookies down and dusted her apron. "Of course, Sweetie. What is it?"

"Why is the bouncy ball so special?" I pointed at the sentence. "This one."

She studied the text, gliding her finger over the large-font letters.

"Well, I think the ball has some sort of meaning to it."

"Meaning?" I raised a brow.

"Yes, meaning." She nodded. "For example, your duck-"

"Marvin?"

She caught her tongue.

"Yes… Marvin. He might be a regular duck to someone else, but to you, he's a friend-"

"He's a bully," I interjected.

My mother began to chuckle. "Oh dear, I hope not."

Her hair fell in front of her eyes. People would classify it as strawberry blonde with hints of pure gold. She moved it back behind her pierced ears.

"Whether he's a bully or a friend, he has some sort of meaning to your life, does he not? If I were to take him away one day, wouldn't you miss him dearly?"

I pondered on her question. I guessed I would miss him. He could be a pain sometimes, but he was mostly tolerable.

"I mean, I guess I'd miss Marvin."

My mother's pearly white teeth showed through her dark-red tinted lips.

"You'll understand one day." She gave me a short hug, squeezing me as tightly as possible before releasing her grip. "If you finish up your work quick enough, you could probably catch your father before he goes into town."

I pulled away.

"Really?" I asked, ready to pounce on the next assignment.

"I gave your father the task of getting me a few groceries, but I feel like you'd be the best candidate to fulfil that chore. Can I trust you in getting me a can of green beans and bologna?" She handed me the grocery list, which had been tucked away in her side pocket.

"You can count on me," I assured her.

She smiled, rustling my hair with her hand.

The ringing of bells stole our attention. My father walked in powdered head to toe in snow. He had a wide smile on his face, revealing his coffee stained teeth. My mother seemed to pick up on something I didn't. She ran up to my father, embracing him. She was lifted off of the floor into my father's arms, laughing as they spun. I peeked my head over the couch, watching them curiously.

I noticed something glistening on both of their cheeks. My mother grazed her hand against my father's face, smiling to no end. Then, they kissed.

I shielded my eyes, falling into the cushions of the couch. I made my gagging noises, exaggerating the motion of throwing up. When I assumed they were finished, I lifted my head back up. Their attention turned to me.

"I think we grossed him out," my mother giggled.

"Should I tell him?" My father turned toward my mother.

"Maybe make it a surprise," she replied, oblivious to the fact that they were standing a few feet away. "Okay, I'll explain to him."

My mother faced me again, clutching my father's hand.

"Your father got the job in New Jersey!" she exclaimed.

Her eyes lit up with such love and passion for my father getting the new job. She loved him, and I could feel it. The love was so apparent you could basically see and smell it in the air. It smelled like fresh roses mixed with chocolate chip cookies, glowing in a pink aura around my parents. She gave my father another kiss, but this time, it was on the cheek.

"You're going to New Jersey…?" my small voice arose.

Truth be told, I didn't want to lose my father. I felt somewhat selfish for wanting him to stay here. It just didn't seem right for him to leave.

My father crouched down in front of me.

"Yes, I'll be going to New Jersey for a couple of weeks to finalize everything. Until I come back, I need you to stay here and protect your mother, okay?"

"Okay," I replied.

He looked back at my mother, who was still gleaming with happiness, then looked back at me.

"Today's a good day, Clyde. Let's make the best of it," he said.

I nodded and let out a sounding, "Okay."

Chapter Three

The Sweet Tooth

To celebrate my father's new job, the whole family hopped in the old blue Chevy pick-up truck and headed downtown. My mother wanted to get a cake to accompany our dinner that night. I'm not going to lie, I was a little nervous when I heard the night's menu. She decided to sear up a juicy sirloin steak, which was a pretty penny out of their wallets.

"Should I invite Sherrill Bleu for dinner? Oh, she's very lovely, and she'll cut us a discount for the cake." My mother glossed her lips with cherry flavored chapstick as she spoke.

"Do we have the budget for an extra plate?" My father glanced at his wallet jammed in the cupholder. "I'm sure Clyde wouldn't mind sharing his plate with… uh…hm, what's their daughter's name?"

I had only seen their daughter once before. However, I didn't catch her name.

"It's Madeline, Honey," my mother answered.

Madeline. I began to picture her face. To my memory, she was a brunette. Her eyes resembled the color of chestnuts. Her skin had been tanned due to her family's beach trip. I remembered her as being taller than me. She never rubbed it in my face or anything; in fact, she was fairly quiet.

"Madeline's a sweet girl. Do you remember Madeline, Clyde?" My father looked at me in the mirror.

I looked away and sighed, my breath frosting the window.

"I don't want anyone to come over."

My mother turned her head, surprised by my reply.

"Why not, Sweetie?"

"Just because…" I turned my attention toward an oncoming billboard advertisement. "Hey, it's Madeline!"

Her face was plastered on a large sign standing at least 20 feet high. She had a wide grin with few gaps from missing teeth. Frosting was swiped across her cheeks and forehead, and her hair was powdered with baking flour. The background was baby blue with black polka dots, and written in giant letters was *Bleu's Bakery's* slogan: *THIS SWEET TOOTH SMILE COULD BE YOURS!*

"Honey, would you look at that? Isn't Sherrill's daughter adorable?" My mother exclaimed. "Clyde, doesn't that make you want to eat some sweets?"

She glanced at me through the mirror.

"But I want to keep my teeth," I said.

"Clyde!" She gasped.

My father hunched his shoulders forward as he attempted to contain his laughter. A light smack on his shoulder and a stern glance from my mother quickly shut him up.

"That's not polite, Clyde. Just be glad you didn't say it in front of her," she scolded and then faced forward.

The silence returned inside the truck. Increasingly, more cars passed by us the closer we got to town. My father switched on the radio. A few channels were filled with loud static while others had some sort of broadcaster shouting into the microphone. We settled on a station which played indie rock music around the clock.

I felt a bit guilty for not agreeing with my mother. She seemed pretty upset with my response, sighing every so often.

As we got closer to downtown, more and more cars began to appear alongside the main road. Although our town was pretty small, there were plenty of visitors from neighboring areas. I guess they thought the tiny shops along the sidewalks were quaint and tourist worthy. There were a few boutiques, but I never went inside any of them. My mother would come home with a few dresses from *Gracie's Boutique*, but that was only during special occasions.

My father parked his truck in a slanted parking spot beside the main road. We made our first stop at *Martin's* for the steak. Immediately when I walked through the entrance, I was hit with the smell of freshly baked bread. The chatter was kept at a low volume. The rustling of paper bags and beeping of scanners filled in most of the silence. We received a few strange looks from the workers as we entered. As we made our way over to the meat section, my mother paused to inspect some vegetables.

"These are bruised, Sweetie. Do you think the other place on Dixon Road has better squash?"

"Dixon Road is a far walk. I'd rather not tire out Clyde. He gets cranky when he's tired," Father said, jutting his thumb in my direction.

"I do not!" I contended loudly.

My parents grinned, turning their faces away from my view; however, I could see their shoulders tense from them attempting to hold back their laughter.

I shook my head, jamming my hands into my coat pocket. From the corner of my eye, I spotted a blurry flash of yellow scurrying across an aisle. I slipped away from my distracted mother and father to find the source of the blurry flash. I peeked around the corner. Searching through the countless containers of gummy candies and jawbreakers, Annalise stood in the middle of Aisle 19, emitting a blinding aura. I hid behind the boxes of cereal conveniently placed on the outer shelves. She held a small brown paper bag in her mitten-covered hands. It took her a few seconds to decide which candy to get. A fitting choice, she shoveled colorful gummy butterflies into her bag. I, personally, would go for the lego blocks candy or green army men gummies.

"Clyde!" My father called.

Annalise whipped her head around to my direction. I sharply turned away, fleeing to my parents.

"What did we say about leaving without us knowing? You know better than to walk away without telling us," Mother chided.

I glanced behind me to assure that Annalise hadn't seen me. I didn't see her blonde locks bouncing as she walked. I figured my cover hadn't been blown.

Father tapped my mother's shoulder and gave her a reminder to pick up a cake from *Bleu's Bakery*. My mother quickly grabbed the cheapest sirloin steak pack and headed to the cashier. I hid behind my parents, careful not to make myself stand out, but I hadn't seen Annalise since I spotted her in the candy aisle. If she saw me, she'd probably ask about the letter. Well, that is, if she had received the letter. What if she didn't get it? Or worse, what if she had thrown it away?

"You okay there, Buddy? You've been awfully quiet," my father nudged my shoulder.

"Uh—yeah. I'm okay." I took a quick glance at Aisle 19. "Can I go get some candy?"

My parents exchanged looks.

"I'll take him," my father volunteered.

He accompanied me to the candy aisle. I was nervous to see Annalise—or for her to see me. I was afraid she had forgotten about me already. I had only just met her and not for that long. I doubted she had even read my heart-filled letter.

We turned the corner into the aisle, and to my dismay, the aisle was empty. Annalise was nowhere to be seen. I didn't see her bright yellow mittens. I couldn't feel the warmth from her radiant aura. In fact, without her there, the aisle felt cold and empty.

"I changed my mind. I don't want any candy."

Without another word, my father and I turned around and headed out the rattling automatic doors to join my mother. My mother anxiously pulled the strap of her faux-feather purse, ready to spill to Sherrill, the flamboyant mother of Madeline and co-owner of *Bleu's Bakery*, about Father's new job. I could hear the loose change dancing around inside her bag as the heels of her boots clicked on the pavement. It became increasingly difficult to walk gracefully on the icy sidewalks. The crystals of melting salt helped us safely make our way inside the bakery.

"Is that Lorraine Whittaker I see?" A lady wearing a blue apron pushed through the swinging doors.

She referred to my mother's first name as only those that weren't my father called her Lorraine. My father referred to my mother as Claire, which was her great-great-grandmother's name.

"Hello, Sherrill! It's been awhile, hasn't it?" My mother gave the lady a warm hug.

Sitting behind the counter, Madeline twirled around in a spinning chair. She wore a giant jean jacket that had far too many holes and was twice her size. I assumed her dark umber hair had been recently cut due to the choppy ends. It had to be cut by either her mother or by herself because no professional stylist would allow that haircut to be roaming the streets. She had a short pixie cut up to her ears and side bangs to go with it.

"What are you looking at?" Madeline stopped spinning in her chair, catching her foot against the shaky counter table.

I flinched at her sudden question.

"My mom saw you on that big sign outside of town," I said, hoping to break the awkward tension.

"What about it?" Her eyes narrowed into a fearless stare, and her body stiffened.

I hesitated, glancing over to my mother, who was still engaged in a conversation with Madeline's mother.

"Um... you have no teeth," I stated.

My mother overheard me making the comment and immediately came over to scold me. She pulled me to the side with a short, sharp tug of the arm and click of the tongue then crouched down in front of me.

"Now, I told you not to say anything about her teeth. You go apologize to Madeline or you get no sweets after dinner." Her pointer finger waved right in my face.

I bit my lower lip and lowered my head, nodding guiltily.

My mother moved aside so I could face Madeline. She didn't seem defensive or offended in any way. In fact, she looked mostly unbothered, returning back to spinning in the chair. She popped a cherry sucker into her mouth, tossing the wrapper into the bin.

I let out a loud sigh before spewing my apology.

"I am *sorry* for making fun of your teeth because you have none," I half heartedly apologized.

I guess it didn't satisfy my parents' expectations. My mother's face turned red as my father's lips tightened together in disappointment and disapproval.

"Oh, don't worry about it. Kids will be kids," Sherril said. "Clyde, why don't you and Madeline go to the arcade for a bit? I'm sure your parents wouldn't mind. It's a safe area."

Madeline and I exchanged looks. She rolled her eyes at her mother's suggestion.

"I like that idea. It'll give us time to catch up." My mother dug inside her purse. "Here's five dollars to exchange for tokens. Try to make them last, please."

I jammed the five dollar bill into my coat pocket. Madeline hopped off the chair and led the way outside. She was still a bit taller than me, but I blamed it on her platform sneakers. She had this sort of bounce when she walked. Her hair bobbed up and down in layers as she moved. She opened the door to the arcade but didn't bother to hold the door for me. Bright neon lights and laser sound effects immediately greeted us upon our arrival. A worker stood behind a glass counter filled with prizes. His fingers were busy texting away. We walked up to the worker, thrusting our fists full of cash toward him. He didn't give a second thought about our ages and handed us a cup filled with 25 tokens each.

"Come with me," Madeline commanded.

I did as told, following closely behind her until we got to the machine titled *Space Invaders*. She dropped in the golden token. Immediately, the screen flashed with the image of a single white rocketship below rows of colorful, block-shaped aliens. Madeline aggressively swiveled the joystick and jammed the red buttons. The flashing images illuminated the dark corner. Tiny rays shot out from the rocketship, eliminating the tiny aliens. She seemed immersed in the game, ignoring my existence entirely. I didn't want to interrupt her focus so I stood idly by, waiting for my turn to play.

"Come on! SHOOT!" She shouted.

It felt a bit weird watching her play. Her hair would occasionally fall in front of her eyes. She'd tuck it behind her ears, but her bangs were merciless.

A worker carrying a tray of pizza on his shoulders passed by. As I stepped aside to allow him to walk through, I caught a glimpse of a familiar object across the room. Yellow mittens were tied at the waist belt of a girl on the other side of the room. I slyly shifted away from the preoccupied Madeline and made my way over to the her. It had to be Annalise. The room grew a few degrees warmer and the yellow mittens seemed to call my name; I swear I could hear them.

The young lady whipped around at the sound of my approaching footsteps, and it was actually Annalise.

Immediately, her wide eyes and bright smile froze me in my place. She threw her arms around me in a sudden embrace. I felt my cheeks get red hot.

She pulled away, digging in her pockets for something.

"Your letter—" She unfolded a piece of paper "— I really like it."

I felt my heart drop as soon as I saw the heart sticker taped across the overlapping flaps. The letter seemed almost untouched. There wasn't a messy crumple or wrinkle in sight.

"Why didn't you correct me when I called you Tom?" She held up the letter, pointing at the bottom.

"Well... you were already so far, and the wind was really loud..." I said bleakly, trying to excuse my behavior.

"*Clyde*. Did I say that right?"

"Perfectly," I uttered.

She flashed a wide smile. That smile could have charmed the most cold-hearted scrooge in the world. I couldn't take my eyes off of her. It felt as if I only had that one second to be with her before she'd leave forever, and I didn't want her to go.

"Who is she? The girl you were talking to?" Annalise asked.

I turned around to see Madeline still preoccupied with the arcade game. She didn't seem to notice my disappearance.

"Oh, her?" I pointed behind me. "I just met her."

"Let me introduce myself, then." Annalise tugged on my arm, pulling me toward Madeline.

I used the rubber soles of my shoes to grip against the carpet.

"No!" I shouted abruptly.

She released my arm and stepped back. I could tell she felt a bit embarrassed. Her cheeks began to blush into a bright red hue.

"I'm sorry. I didn't mean to scare you…" I apologized.

"It's fine. I shouldn't have just pulled you like that." She looked downward. "I think my mother wants me home. I'll see you later, okay?"

I bit my lower lip. It was obvious she was trying to avoid any sort of eye contact. I was sure she didn't want to see me anymore, but I wasn't sure if I was ready to let her go so soon.

"I have something to give you, but it's at home! Can I meet you later today?" I almost begged.

She twiddled her thumbs together. I couldn't read her facial expression as a definite yes or no. She seemed to be chewing on the insides of her cheek, deciding whether or not to accept my offer.

"Alright. Meet me later tonight." She finally lifted her head, looking me directly in the eyes.

I fell into another trance, almost forgetting to tell her the location. I wasn't sure if I could sneak out to see her given that my parents were in a celebratory mood.

"Can you meet me at my house? It's the brown one at the end of the road. Meet me at eight o'clock, okay?"

She charmingly laughed. "Okay, I'll see you then."

Her voluminous hair bounced as she swung around. Before she exited the building, she put on her yellow mittens and gave one last glance toward me then pushed through the door. The sunlight gathered around her. Just like that, she was gone.

"Hey, stupid. What are you looking at?" Madeline burst the intimate bubble with her blunt but sharp nature.

"Nothing," I snarled.

Her eyebrows furrowed as her top lip pulled upward, sneering at my rude reply. Without a second thought, she snatched my upper arm, pulling me toward another machine. The game titled *Dance Dance Revolution* played clamorous techno music, occasionally shouting congratulatory remarks. It was overwhelming to say the least. I placed my cup on a flat surface, then stood on the platform covered in squares with arrows inside of them.

"I can't dance," I stated.

"You don't actually dance, dummy. You step on arrows." She popped in two tokens. "My treat."

We stood on each side of the platform. As she went through the list of songs, I wondered what it would have been like if Annalise had met Madeline. I doubted she would have liked Annalise. They seemed to be polar opposites. Madeline most likely became the school's bully at her school while Annalise was class president. Madeline was too aggressive for Annalise, anyways. She was the soul-sucking grouch to the giddy elmo. It was best if they didn't meet.

"Okay. Just step on the boxes that have the same arrows as on the screen." She stepped upon the center box with two footprints on it. "Get ready. It's about to start."

A giant message flashed onto the screen: **START**. Colorful arrows came up from the bottom of the screen. The first red arrow pointed to the right. I stepped on the corresponding box. **PERFECT!** The next green arrow pointed straight. I stepped on that one too. **GREAT!**

I eventually got the hang of it. In my opinion, I think I did way better than the she-devil next to me. The arrows flew by like a breeze. The words *PERFECT* and *GREAT* didn't even sound like real words to me anymore.

The song ended and our scores were finally posted. I scored a triple A+ while Madeline scored only a double A+. She gave me a glare and then snatched my coin cup. She took out two tokens and inserted them into the slot. The game lit up again.

"I'm getting pretty tired. I think I'm going to go back to the store," I said, stepping off the platform.

She suddenly turned her head toward me. She looked as if I murdered her pet snake, which I assumed she had because of how scary she was. I thought I would never feel this feeling with another person. Captivated, I would describe it as. Her mouth was slightly gaped open. Behind her stray hairs, her hidden eyes were enticing me to stay. It made the hairs stand up on the back of my neck. An upsetting feeling sprouted in my stomach.

I shook my head then stepped back onto the platform. "Okay, one more game. That's it."

She seemed a bit shocked. It was like she didn't expect me to stay. Did she even want me to stay?

"It's not like I wanted you to stay or anything. Be free to leave whenever you want." Her face then turned sour, back to her usual self.

I chose the song this time. All the songs on the game's playlist were foreign to me. I just chose the song with the easiest beat and shortest time length.

Madeline readied herself. Her legs were locked in position. I spotted her eyeing the arrows on my side and suspected some foul play beforehand. Maybe she'd try to shove me or try to step on my arrows to throw off my points. I kept a sharp eye on her dangerous plays.

When the song started, the arrows came up faster than the last game. It was a bit more complicated, throwing in more combinations than the last. I no longer saw the *"PERFECT's"* and the *"GREAT's"*. Rather, all I got was *"GOOD"* and occasional *"MISS"*. I danced my heart out for this song. I couldn't even break focus to keep an eye on Madeline. She seemed to be doing well on her own, getting almost all of the combinations. It was challenging keeping up with her, but I couldn't admit my defeat.

"I won! You see that?" She pointed at the double A+ on her score results. "And *you* lost."

My score of D+ flashed repetitively on the screen.

"Yeah, so what? I beat you the first time," I contested.

She wouldn't give it up. She reached to grab the token cup, but I stopped her.

"I said one round!" I snatched my cup away. "I have to, uh… go somewhere. We can play again and break the tie. I'll be better by then. Way better!"

She put on her usual pout and rolled her eyes. "Whatever. Leave if you must…"

Her arms crossed over her chest, and her back turned to me. It was tempting. I would have inserted another coin if it wasn't for the meeting with Annalise later on, but I was sure Madeline could handle herself. She seemed pretty tough on her own.

"Next time, if you win, I'll…" I pondered on the punishment. "… I'll hold your hand!"

Her face changed to disgust. "I don't want to touch you. Boys are icky!"

Not going to lie, I was slightly hurt by her comment. I thought I had made a meaningful impact on her life by this good hour of hanging out with her.

"Well, what do you think should happen?"

"I think the winner gets to order the loser around for a day." She had that answer in her back pocket since the moment we walked in. "And you can't say no!"

I figured this was the only way I could escape without feeling guilty.

"Deal."

We both shook hands and then emptied the golden tokens into our pockets. The plastic cups were then tossed into the trash can by the door. Before we left, we waved goodbye to the worker behind the counter, who didn't notice us leaving due to his attention being directed at his cellphone. We could have taken a small prize without him noticing, but we didn't.

As soon as we exited the arcade, our parents walked through the doors of the bakery. Madeline left me in the dust, running to her mother. I followed behind to my own parents, the coins rattling inside my pockets. Occasionally, my coat would slide off my shoulders from the tokens weighing it down. I would fix my coat to have it slide off again in an endless cycle.

"Did you guys have fun?" Madeline's mother asked.

"No," she stated. "He's pretty boring, and he sucks at playing games."

She stuck her tongue out at me, and boy, it made my blood boil. I had so many things to say about her right in front of her parents' faces, but I held my tongue.

"We can set up another playdate with these two, and hopefully, it won't be so bad next time," my mother said. "Well, it's getting kinda late. I think it's best if we head out."

The two mothers exchanged their goodbyes. All Madeline and I did was give each other nasty looks, but that within itself was enough. We left promptly afterward. The streets became heavily packed with cars. I noticed a few of their license plates were from other states. Some were even as far as Florida. I felt possessive of my town. It felt a bit weird having people from outside of Pennsylvania visit such a small area. New business would flood the empty buildings, drawing in more people. Still, the road leading to our house remained mostly bare. No visitors passed through that part of town.

I waited for my father to open the door for me before getting in the truck. His shoulders would tense when I swing the door too wide in fear that I would hit the car in the space next to us. If anything, his wallet sweat more than he did. I didn't complain and hopped into my seat, pulling the seat belt across my chest and buckling it in. The door unintentionally slammed shut. Dad started the engine. A few people passed by behind us. When the coast was clear, my father backed out, putting one hand on the steering wheel and the other on the headpost of the passenger seat. I ducked my head to allow him to see the back clearly. We pulled away, nearly hitting the car next to us. My father wasn't the best driver, and my mother often reminded him of that. She gave him the benefit of the doubt for now and kept her comments to herself.

I bounced my leg up and down frantically. The car ride felt incredibly slow, each car seemed to be creeping by. It gave me ample time to catch the specifics of those cars. The yellow Punch Buggy held a family of four whose children, around the same age as me, played with their gameboys in the backseat. A giant man drove the next car, a reddish-brown van, with both of his hands gripping the leather steering wheel. He wore dark-rimmed glasses and had little to no hair on his head. We made awkward eye contact, both of us then averting our eyes right away.

I closed my eyes, hoping that when I opened them again, we'll be pulling into our driveway. Unfortunately, that didn't happen. We made our way out of the inner town and headed for the back roads.

"When are we getting home?" I asked, rather impatiently.

"In a few. Just be patient," my mother replied.

I pouted, not exactly satisfied with her answer. The clock seemed to be ticking by fast. Any minute, it would turn to eight o'clock, and I'd be late to meet with Annalise. I fidgeted with the buttons on my coat, twisting and turning one, slipping it in and out of the loop, and tugging until the strings that bound it to the fabric ripped apart. I sharply looked at my mother, sighing with relief that my crime went unnoticed. I slipped the loose button into my coat pocket, acting as if nothing had happened. My hands began to get clammy. I wiped them across my jeans. The truck's engine roared louder as Dad pressed harder on the gas pedal. My heart rate increased the faster he sped up.

"Honey, slow down. It's icy," Mother demanded.

My father lightened upon the gas pedal, allowing the truck to slow down. I straightened up, leaning at the edge of my seat. I didn't want him to slow down. If anything, I wanted him to speed up. I pictured Annalise waiting outside in the cold with her mittens rubbing together frantically, her breath forming into a cloud of fog. I pictured Annalise's patience running low. She wanted to go home. She didn't want to wait for me anymore.

"Are we almost there?" I almosted begged.

My father's hand lifted off of the steering wheel, pointing his finger upward. "In just a minute, Clyde. Be patient."

I couldn't be patient. I squirmed in my seat, ready to hop out of it any second. We passed by a familiar tree. I recognized the bare body, exposing the reddish rings. If my memory didn't deceive me, we were fairly close. Another tree passed by. Then, the woods appeared.

My eyes widened at the sight of our burnt sienna-colored house. The driveway had accumulated a good bit of snow since we left. We pulled in and parked under the canopy. I unbuckled my seatbelt, releasing it. The spool ate up the seatbelt, swinging the metal buckle into the window, nearly cracking it. Both my mother and father turned away, ready to scold me.

"I get our car is not the fanciest, but you don't have to break it." My father shook his head.

"Sorry…" I mumbled.

I opened the truck door and helped myself out. A bit of mud splashed onto the side of the truck as I plopped onto the icy grass. We locked the car door and headed inside. My muddy boots were placed in the cubby. I threw my coat on the rack and ran upstairs. After barging into my room, I searched the drawers for a special item to give to Annalise. I began to get nervous about filling the bluff I created with my "preplanned" present to her. Each item I stumbled across lacked any personal value. I considered giving away Marvin, but I doubted he would have appreciated that. If anything, he'd nag her head off. I also considered giving away a few of my army men, but I doubted she would have liked them.

I flipped over a few pillows on my bed and kicked away loose articles of clothing that laid on the floor. There were no hidden pieces of candy or plastic rings. I took a second to look around the room as a whole.

The sheen of the velvet caught the corner of my eye. I felt my heart drop for a second. It wasn't right for me to give it away, but it seemed the most fitting.

I grabbed the velvet box and twisted the latch to open it. Inside, the colorful block rested peacefully. I swiped my hand across the window to see if anyone stood outside. I still had a good hour before eight. I set the box down onto the table with the Rubik's Cube in hand and then made my way out the door. I trotted down the stairs and stopped near the opening of the kitchen where my parents were.

My mother marinated sirloin steak while my father chopped up a few vegetables to stir fry. *The Temptations* played on the stereo. I believe the song playing was *Since I Lost My Baby*. A smile was plastered across my mother's face. She swayed to the tune of the music, closing her eyes to take it all in. My father did the same. He mouthed the lyrics, bobbing his head to the sound of the trumpets. I saw them take a quick look at each other in the midst of preparing dinner. Mom washed her hands, dried them, then walked over to Dad. She wrapped her slim arms around his waist, giggling before resting her head against his upper back. He wiped his hands with a rag and then turned around to return the hug. They separated, but still remained close, my father leaning against the kitchen counter for support. He placed his hands on her waist, and she placed hers on his shoulders. They danced around the kitchen, refusing to break eye contact.

"*Since I lost my baby... next time, I'll be kinder...*" the lyrics played.

He took her hand and spun her around as the chorus came in. Mid-spin, my mother spotted me standing in the frame of the door. They both paused then waved their hands for me to join them. I hurried over, accepting my mother and father's invitation. The song changed. *My Girl* played on the stereo. This threw my parents into a joyous fit. They spun me around, lifting me off the floor at times. It felt like I was flying, taking control of my life away. I would describe it as freeing. My father snapped his fingers while tapping his foot to the beat.

"Hey… hey… hey!" he sang.

My mother covered her mouth, laughing at his attempt at matching the melody. He ignored our ridiculing and continued on. A certain persona possessed him. He had much more confidence and swagger. My mother fell for it all. As the music slowed, they came together again, kissing each other on the lips. I shielded my eyes, making a loud gagging noise. Before looking back, I heard my parents giggle. Dad lifted me up in the air, spinning me around as the song ended. I was then placed down on the floor.

"Alright, we had our fun. I think we need to get dinner going," my mother said while still giggling.

The radio still played as they returned to their duties. My mother hummed the tune, softly swaying as she put the steak into plastic baggies. I took a seat at the kitchen table where I could see outside of the living room window. No one stood outside of the fence nor on my porch. I opened up *The Giver* from where my mother left off to distract myself. However, I couldn't exactly read every word on the page. Some words were beyond my vocabulary, but I didn't want anyone to know that. Truth be told, the cover of the book drew me in. It had the face of an old man sulking with a ripped off corner, exposing the silhouette of trees during sundown. I had no idea what the plot of the book was, but from the image, I could almost sympathize with the old man. I vowed to myself that I'd come back to read it sometime in the future.

I took another look outside of the window. Annalise was nowhere in sight. I set the book back onto the table and hopped out of my seat. My father placed the vegetables into a straining bowl then placed the bowl into the sink. He washed the vegetables thoroughly, accidentally splashing water all over the kitchen floor.

"I need to get something from outside. I'll put on my coat!" I stated.

My mother sighed. "You've been outside enough."

"Please! 10 minutes!" I pleaded.

"Clyde, you're going to get sick." My father dried his hands on a white dish rag then wiped his hands on his pants.

"Okay, just 10 minutes." I held up my hands to show all 10 fingers. "My toys are going to get lost in the snow! And I won't be able to find them!"

A loud *clunk* sounded from the drop of dirty dishes into the sink.

"Seven minutes *only*," Mother firmly emphasized.

I dashed up the stairs to my bedroom, retrieving the Rubik's Cube. I hoped that the effort amounted to more than the presentation because I didn't exactly have anything to put the gift in. I returned down the steps, quicky slipping my arms through my giant coat and pulling on my boots. As I opened the front door, I noticed the angelic beauty standing outside of the fences. She wore a beige coat this time. Thick wool lined the inside of the hood along with the cuffs of the coat and the lower rim. Of course, her trademark yellow mittens covered her dainty hands. She smiled as soon as our eyes met. I couldn't even complete the action of closing the front door just by seeing a single glance of hers. My heart raced. I had to remind myself I only had seven minutes to play outside. I shut the door behind me then ran over to her by the fence.

"Did ya think I would skip out?" she jested.

"I had my doubts... but I'm glad you're here!" I exclaimed.

She giggled, tucking her hair behind her ears.

"Well, where's that thing you had to give me?" She held out her hands. "Or should I close my eyes? Is it a surprise?"

"Surprise...? Yes! Close your eyes," I requested.

She covered her eyes with her dandelion-colored mittens. Being so close, I could see the intricate designs made with cotton thread. A small white flower was embroidered onto the rim of the mittens. I believe they were Calla Lilies. My mom loved those flowers.

I stuck my hand in my right pocket, worried she could see the cube outline through the fabric. Using the feeling I had left in my fingers, I turned a few rows around. I closed my eyes, praying that she'd like the gift then pulled the Rubik's Cube out and rested it in the center of my palm.

"Okay. Open your eyes." I huffed, a cloud of condensation forming in front of me.

The tiny specks of white dust collected on her lashes. She batted her eyes, squinting from the transition of darkness to pure white. I couldn't read how she felt about the gift. There wasn't a particular expression at first. She just kinda stared at it. Her hands reached out to grab it. I guess the object was as foreign to her as it was to me.

"Wha-What is it?" She asked, holding it in her hands.

"It's a Rubik's Cube. You turn the rows around and like… well, that's about it."

To be completely honest, I had already forgotten what the end goal for the cube was. Turning the blocks around seemed entertaining enough.

Annalise continued inspecting the object with very little to no expression.

"You… hate it, don't you…" I said.

Her head jolted upward, turning side to side. "No! That's not–I mean, that's not what I am saying. I just–"

She stopped her thought.

"It's fine. You don't have to like it. I didn't expect you to anyways."

"Sorry. I'm not very good with my words. I'm just really grateful," she said. " I like it, Clyde. I like it a lot."

The comment took me off guard. I felt my cheeks beginning to blush. She noticed them, too, and smiled.

"You look like a cherry, Clyde," she teased.

I covered my cheeks with my hands. It was a bit embarrassing for her to notice. It reminded me of how my mother used to always point out my red cheeks, especially in front of others. It would just make them redder most times.

"Don't sweat it. Here." Annalise removed her mittens, handing them to me.

I pushed them away, shaking my head, no.

"Come on. Your hands are probably freezing." She thrust the mittens forward.

"I-I don't want them. You should keep them since they're yours," I said.

She frowned, still holding the yellow mittens in her hands. She then shrugged and put them back on.

"Another time, I guess," she sighed.

I smiled.

There would be another time.

Her arm lifted to expose the watch around her wrist. It had been seven minutes.

"I have to get home. It was nice seeing you again!" She bent over the short fence, embracing me in her arms.

Although it was probably 15 degrees outside, I had never felt so warm. I didn't want us to part ways, but I knew we had to. She let go of me.

"See you later?" She tilted her head, batting her eyes again.

"Okay."

It was an invitation I couldn't turn down, and I'm sure she realized that. She took a couple of steps backwards before turning around and walking away. Occasionally, she'd take a glance back one or two times, but after the snow began to pick up, I couldn't see her bouncy blonde curls or her yellow mittens anymore. I didn't want to go back inside in hopes of her returning for one last hug, but I felt my mother and father's anxious knee bouncing from behind the wooden front door. I turned away, painstakingly walking back to the front porch. The winds howled as I trudged through the dunes of snow. Maybe they were taunting me for my gift. I didn't mind.

The doors swung open before I would get my icy hands on the doorknob. My mother's mouth gaped slightly open upon seeing me standing on the other side. She stepped aside to let me in. I kicked my boots against the house to shake off the excess snow and walked inside. My coat was taken from my arms and thrown on the rack, and my shoes were unlaced and placed in the cubby. There were a few *crackles* of oil before the searing took place from the steak being laid down into the pan. The house smelled of partially burnt garlic and thyme. The kitchen fan blew a few papers from my father's desk onto the floor, scattering them across the carpet. The stereo had been completely shut off and sat lifelessly on the table. Just like that, my short visit with Annalise was finished, and in an unpredictable amount of time, I knew that I was going to see her again.

Chapter Four

❄

Strangers

I STOOD IN A CROWD of blurry faces. *Strangers*. They had no eyes, no noses, and no mouths, wandering around and occasionally bumping into each other. *No emotions*. I couldn't recognize anyone. All were faceless strangers with no purpose. Their clothing consisted of gray, loose coverings. The buildings which towered over us were dull and bare. They had no windows to peer through and no doors to enter. They were just stiff, desolate structures.

None of the faceless strangers seemed to notice me. Some would bump into me and move on. Others would avoid me entirely. I searched for my parents throughout the crowd, the faceless bodies seemingly growing into the hundreds the further I dug into it. My personal space began to shrink as more bodies appeared. It got to the point where I couldn't even see a clear view of the sky. All I saw were the nameless, faceless strangers. I felt my throat tighten. The strangers were relentless. They shoved me along their path. I had no choice but to follow them. Even when their pushing caused me to fall, they yanked me back up to my feet and dragged me along with them. I wanted to call out for my parents and tell them I was here, but the faceless strangers would silently condemn me every time a whimper would let out.

The crowd shifted over to an empty square of burnt grass. A faceless girl around my height danced in the center. No one paid any attention to her except for me, and no one else could see her except for me. She brought her arms up into the air above her head then spun around. Her gray coverings floated up to her thighs before dropping softly. She let her arms down beside her waist, cocking her head upward like a bird. Her foot lifted to her knee, and her arms raised once more, reaching toward the sky. Her fingers straightened until she couldn't reach any further. She collapsed onto her knees in the charred grass. Black soot dirtied her dress. Her shoulders began to stiffen. She took her hand and wiped away a nonexistent tear. Again and again, she swiped her hand under the area where her tears would have fallen. I pushed passed the crowd and walked toward her. Her head lifted in my direction. She could only hear my footsteps, but she wasn't frightened by them.

"Do I know you?" I asked.

The crowd jumped at the sound of my voice, scurrying around in search of its source. I dropped to the floor as did the girl. The faceless bodies sharply twisted and turned, using their hands as their eyes to find the source of the voice. She placed her finger against the area where her mouth would have been as to say *hush*.

I nodded, though she couldn't see it.

Her right hand slid against the ground, powdering it with black soot. She then held it out for me to accept. The wind settled down into a cooing *purr*. The faceless strangers were at a standstill. Not a rustle of leaves nor footsteps sounded in the midst of the invitation given by the faceless girl. My arms seemed to have added some weight. It became heavier and heavier for me to lift it. I wanted to grab her hand, but I couldn't. She fully stood up, peering down at me for a mere second, then fled. I chased after her. The still bodies snapped into action, grabbing and tugging at my limbs. Their icy cold hands wrapped around my arm, pulling me in the opposite direction. A few would grab at my hair and face, beckoning me to stay. I didn't want to stay with them. I was afraid of them. I eventually broke through the crowd and ran into an empty alleyway. The girl stood in the middle, swaying her hips. When she heard me approaching, she'd dash in the opposite direction. Whenever she was far enough away, she'd taunt me, pausing to bow or wave. It would give me time to catch up, but I could never be fully with her. When I thought I could finally reach out and just touch her hand, she turned the corner. I sped up to catch her, but when I whipped around the sharp bend, all I saw was the spitting image of myself. There was no girl. She had never existed.

Chapter Five

In the spur of the moment

It had been a week since I saw Annalise. The days seemed to pass by slowly with no incentive to carry them. I'd watch the car lights break through the cracks in the blinds then diminish as their tires rolled over the mountains of frozen ice on the damp pavement. I guess the loneliness caught up with me. The world seemed to reach a standstill. Then, all of a sudden, everything resumed. After my father left to visit his new job location in New Jersey, the sunlight began peeking through the clouds more often. The subtle green showed through the translucent layers of sleet which rested on top of the frozen blades of grass. I could have sworn I saw a sprouting Lily in the midst of the beaten shrubs. In all honesty, I couldn't let go of this season for some reason. I had rolled up a miniature snowman and placed it in my freezer because I thought I could preserve a small piece of winter, but it ended up melting less than 30 minutes later. The melted snow water leaked from the freezer onto the floor. It wasn't the best surprise for my mother to find.

The vacuum roared as it was rolled across the dusty carpet. My mother hummed a familiar tune—one that I couldn't quite put my finger on. She wore one of the dresses from *Gracie's Boutique*, the lavender one with the ruffled seam stitching at the end of the dress. Her side bangs swept across the left side of her face, elegantly falling beyond her shoulders. The glare of sunlight reflected off of her wristwatch, flickering on and off as she dragged the vacuum back and forth. Her pink-dusted eyelids receded as she looked upward. She shut off the noisy cleaning device.

"Are you just going to stare out the window all day or are you going to help me clean the house?" my mother asked, yanking the cord from the wall socket.

"I'll help you…" I slid off the couch.

She ordered me to lift the rug up for her to sweep under. These places were usually ignored during her cleaning. I wondered why she gave them so much attention now. When she turned her back, I peered into the kitchen to see a piping hot kettle of boiling water on the stove with fresh bread slices crisping into the toaster. A bottle of jam sat on the table with the fake lilies placed in a clear vase of water.

"In a bit, you need to head up and change. Sherrill is coming over for brunch. I think Madeline is joining us also," she informed me.

I dropped the rug, causing a large wave of dust to emanate from under it. My mother fanned the air, coughing into the crease in her elbow. Her eyes began to water as did mine. Before I could even come up with an apology, she ran into the kitchen to dust off her dress. I couldn't blame her. The dress was a gift from my dad for their wedding anniversary. She almost didn't want to remove the price tag to reserve every bit of sentiment from the thoughtful gift.

"Clyde! That wasn't very nice of you to do that. The dust is everywhere, and I have to clean it up!" she scolded from the kitchen.

I panicked and darted toward the broom to begin sweeping up the mess I had made. She held out her hand to stop me. With her eyes closed, she flicked her wrist to shoo me away. I obeyed and stepped away. She lifted her head to prevent any stray tears from falling and ruining her makeup.

"Go change, please. They'll be here in a bit." My mother gained her composure.

I headed upstairs and into my bedroom. In total honesty, I still felt a little flustered from seeing Madeline. I wasn't sure why. She was the exact opposite of Annalise. Her hair wasn't as well kempt, and her skin didn't glow as brightly. She had rude manners on top of that. Nonetheless, I dug into my piles of clothes to find the freshest outfit I could find. There were khakis reserved for special house parties and restaurant dinners on the weekends; luckily, they hadn't been worn in ages. I also found the sweater that had the fewest holes in the fabric. My grandmother had given me this sweater. It was burgundy with a small flowery symbol embroidered on the breast pocket.

The house phone's blaring ringtone echoed throughout the house. I had a feeling that my father was on the end of the line. I dashed out my bedroom door to the closest phone and picked it up.

"Hello?" I said.

"Hey, Sport. How's it going over there?" my father answered.

His voice sounded raspier, yet it held hints of joy.

"It's going okay. Me and mom miss you." I lifted the phone closer to my face. "When are you coming back?"

There was a short pause.

"I... I wouldn't count on me being home by the end of this week. The weather sure is a fighter out here in New Jersey. Do me a favor? Take good care of your mother for me. I'll be home by next Monday for sure."

I pursed my lips. It had been a solid three days without my father's presence in the household. I guess my mother felt the loneliness, too. We almost never invited people over to our house.

"About mom... She's getting um... She's inviting *people over*..." I lowered my voice near the end. "I think she's going crazy, too!"

"Crazy? I guess I have to head home a lot sooner. How crazy is she, Son?"

I smiled at the thought of my plan working. I wanted him home as quickly as possible.

"She's wearing that dress that you bought her, and—and she put fake flowers in the vase. I think she's trying to impress Mrs. Bleu."

"Oh, well, I'm putting you in charge of making sure she isn't going completely mad by the time I come back. Can I trust you with that task?"

The wind seemed to pick up on the other end of the line. It became harder to hear him.

"You can trust me!" I shouted.

"Oka— let me spea—mother—" the call cut off my father's words.

I wasn't sure what to do. After a few seconds of silence from my father, I slammed the phone back into the port and ran into my room again.

A burgundy minivan with the logo **Bleu's Bakery** plastered on the sides pulled into the driveway. I could see Madeline's pout through the window with her arms crossed at her chest. Even through the stubborn frost on the glass, I could see the bright shade of red smeared across her mother's lips. Mrs. Bleu's pouf light grazed the car's rooftop. She lowered her head as she exited the minivan, being careful not to mess up her new do.

I moved away from the window and took in the view of my room. Toys were scattered all over the carpet. A few articles of clothing hung out of the hamper; I hoped those were the clean ones. My bed had been made this morning by my mother, but shortly after she left my room, I tore the bed apart in search of my missing army men. I heard footsteps approaching the front door, then the knocking sounded. I raced to throw the mess under my bed and into other small crevices. My mother opened the door. I heard the kind greeting of Mrs. Bleu. I stuffed the clothes deep inside the hamper and covered it with the lid. The rustled sheets were hidden by my blanket, neatly tucked into the edges of the bed frame. My mother stepped toward the staircase, ready to call for me to come down. I opened my desk drawer and slid the unlidded pens and scrap paper into it.

"Clyde! Come down! Madeline is here!" My mother announced.

I headed for the door but stopped at the mirror. I must have twisted and turned something fierce that night because my hair was an absolute mess. I couldn't be seen like this. I grabbed the beanie from under my bed and slipped it on my head. I heard the creak of the first step, signaling that Mom was coming up to retrieve me. I straightened my slightly wrinkled shirt and rolled up the cuffs on my worn out jeans.

My mother, with a stern look on her face, opened the door. She immediately went into her motherly position, placing her hands on her hips and waiting for me to answer for myself. Of course, I pretended I didn't hear her the first time she called and walked passed her down the steps. Mrs. Bleu sat in the kitchen with the latest magazine issue opened on the table in front of her. She nibbled on a slice of toast with a little bit of jam spread across it. Madeline sat beside her with a Game Boy in her hands. She had her eyes glued to it, barely paying attention to me as I entered the kitchen.

Mrs. Bleu's eyes lit up as I walked in.

"Is this little Clyde I see? Good afternoon, handsome young man," she greeted. "I brought my sweet daughter, Madeline. I'm sure you guys had a fun time at the arcade. I figured you'd want to hang out a lot more. What do you say, Clyde?"

"I'm sure my son would love that. Who knows? This could become a weekly thing!" My mother answered for me.

She placed her hands upon my shoulders.

I attempted to grab Madeline's attention with a tilt of my head, but whatever she was doing on that small device seemed intense. Her eyebrows furrowed as her thumbs kept busy. She'd violently sway a few times, darting her eyes back and forth across the screen.

"Now, Madeline. What did we talk about in the car? You should have left that toy in the car. My goodness," Mrs. Bleu scolded.

Madeline rolled her eyes and sighed. She was rudely mannered, too. Unbelievable. I bet Annalise wouldn't have done that. I doubted she'd even touch that device.

Mrs. Bleu coughed sharply. She straightened her posture and faced us.

"I hope you don't mind my daughter's awfully rude manners—Madeline, put it away—because I most definitely raised her better than that," she said.

With Madeline's lack of acknowledgement, her mother snatched the device and jammed it into her purse. Madeline finally made eye contact with me, which induced her to make another eyeroll and exaggerated sigh.

"Alright, let's go, loser." She hopped off the chair and dragged me toward the front door.

I stopped in my tracks, holding my ground. She tugged a little harder. I guess she didn't get the memo that I didn't want to go with her.

"Go on, Clyde. The snow won't last much longer. Make the best of it, you two," my mother said, taking a sip from her tea. "Oh! Take her to that spot you like to go to. Sherrill, did I tell you about that plot of land of Tom's? It's really nice."

While they continued on with their mother-to-mother conversations, Madeline and I snuck away. My mother was right. The snow wasn't going to last much longer. It had already melted on the steps. A wave of anxiety came over me. A heavy feeling developed in my chest from the sight of the green grass.

"You look sick. Are you going to hurl?" Madeline commented. "Lemme give you a word of advice: look the other way, Buddy."

"I'm not going to hurl, and if I was going to, I'd make sure it'd cover those pearly white sneakers of yours," I snarled.

"Whatever…" She shrugged it off.

We kicked around the frozen dunes of snow in the driveway. We thought we were doing more good than harm. Our truck's bumper would scrape against the hard snow formations. I hoped that when my father came home, we'd spare him the pain of the ear-wrenching sound of scraping metal. Madeline found a mountainous pile and attempted to kick it down. Her supporting foot slipped out from under her, and with a short yelp, she landed on the slick concrete with a *crack*. I ran over to her immediately, unsure whether to help her or laugh at her. She didn't seem like she was in immense pain; rather, she was in momentary shock. Her arms and legs sprawled out on the ground as she peered up at the clouds.

"Ow…" she groaned.

I took this as a cue to help her up and allowed her to grab my hand. At first, she hesitated but then gave in after she realized she couldn't get up by herself. After we locked hands, I used all my strength to yank her upward. The way she stood looked similar to how Mr. Crocker living down on Mayfield Street stood with his bad back. She complained about the same too.

"Thank you, Mister. That stupid ice block got the best of me. I'll show em' one day," she huffed.

I crushed a few small pieces of ice with the sole of my shoe, twisting my foot as it crunched against the cement. A wispy breeze swept by, revealing a fresh scar going through her left eyebrow. I couldn't help but stare at it. It seemed recent with because of how red the area was. She was quick to notice my gaze and covered the scar with her bangs.

"What happened to you?" I rudely pointed.

Her eyebrows furrowed.

"I fought some bullies at school. They deserved it." She held up a balled fist. "If you think this is bad, wait till you see them…"

I stepped back, holding my hands up. Although she built up an intimidating demeanor, I didn't feel very threatened by her. Those glossy brown eyes held something deeper. I could feel it. Whether she won the fight or not, she didn't leave without taking a toll deeper than the naked eye could see.

"Hey, what's that?" she asked.

As soon as I saw the direction she was heading toward, the object immediately caught my eye. My heart sank into my stomach. The snow softly crunched as she lifted up the object. The brightly-blocked cube rested in the palm of her hands. I wanted to snatch it from her and go somewhere far away like the woods or my own bedroom. My bedroom had a lock on it. No one could get in unless they busted down the door. The woods also held many hiding spots. I couldn't be found there. For sure, no one would look for me. My mother seemed to be deep in conversation with Mrs. Bleu about who knows what. I just wanted to disappear with or without the Rubik's Cube.

"Are…Are you crying? Was this yours?" Madeline held up the toy. "I wasn't going to take it. I just wanted to see…"

I swiped my sleeve across my eyes then jammed my hands into my pockets.

"I'm going back inside." I made my way toward the front door.

Suddenly, a pair of frail arms wrapped around me. She tightened her embrace, snuggling her face against my back. No words were spoken. Even though the sun came out to shine brightly and warm the earth, it felt like we were frozen in time. I didn't need to see her nor hear her to understand what she felt. It was nothing more than an attempt of sympathy for an inscrutable situation. I couldn't even understand my own emotions at the moment.

She pulled away, almost feeling guilty for suddenly embracing me. We didn't say a word to each other. Our eyes held our conversations. We'd blink to say *hello*, again and again, batting our eyelids when the situation humored us.

"Well?" Her brow raised. "Say something, Whittaker."

She called me by my last name and became the only one to do so. I never cherished anything more. It warmed my heart hearing it; though, with the sharp tongue of my mother, the referral to my last name never ended on a good note. Nonetheless, it made me feel oddly safe.

I took a deep breath in. "Come with me."

We marched down to my father's plot of land which so achingly awaited my return. I felt it calling every night from my bedroom. I tried muffling it with my pillows, but it was enticing. Madeline didn't seem to mind it. She seemed almost eager to go. However, the journey wasn't as adventurous as anticipated. I felt it was my duty to spice things up a bit. After all, she was the honorary guest of the house. As my duty as a host, I held the responsibility to entertain said guest.

"Shh…" I placed my finger on my lips. "You have to be very quiet."

"Why?" she whispered.

It took me a second to think of a reply. There were countless options, maybe a fire breathing dragon or a crazed, armored gorilla.

"There's a… Bigfoot! Oh, yes! He's out there…" I crouched down.

Madeline followed close behind me, darting her eyes left and right for the deadly beast. Our steps were thought out, careful for loud twigs and thick sheets of ice. We'd take turns walking in front of the other to equally have each other's back. As we crept along, I noticed a glowing red illuminating the shrubs—then, I immediately knew what was to come.

"The floor is lava! Quick! Get off the ground!" I shouted.

We burst into chaotic panic. Madeline ran to the closest tree and began climbing. She seemed more prepared than I was for this situation. I had never climbed a tree before, so I was a bit hesitant trying to keep up with Madeline. She reached nearly the highest branch and then looked down at me. The sunlight beamed behind her, creating a halo around her head. She didn't seem to be amused by my lack of effort to survive.

"What are you doing down there? Hurry! I see the lava coming!" She warned. "Argh! You're too slow! Let me help you up!"

She crawled down from the top of the tree to lend me a hand. As soon as we locked arms, I began climbing up. The rough bark scraped against my skin as I crawled up the tree. I could feel the light scratches forming under my thin clothing. I thought of them as battle wounds, wiping away the sweat on my forehead as a sign of relief. Madeline also swiped at beads of sweat running down her forehead with an exaggerated huff. I pressed my back against a thick branch and rested my head against the tree.

Madeline loudly gasped, pointing in a certain direction. I sat upward, trailing whatever she was pointing at.

"I think I see him! Bigfoot! He's so furry…" she stared in awe.

A dark furry creature dug in the bushes. If I hadn't known of my neighbor's Bernese Mountain Dog, Charley, I would have thought it was Bigfoot, too. I couldn't burst her bubble. She seemed just as into it as I was. It felt wrong to rob her of her happiness and excitement, so I kept my mouth shut.

"Okay, let's head down. I think the coast is clear," I said, double checking the ground for lava.

I hopped down first, making sure to land in the softest pile of snow to prevent alarming my neighbor's dog. Madeline came down next, landing right next to me. We crept toward the creature with light footsteps. Halfway to the area, the scenery changed before our very eyes.

"Wait! Don't move!" I shouted.

I remembered seeing this setting somewhere in my school books. Below us, we stood on thick floating pieces of ice that separated us from glacial waters, which awaited our plunge. We were surrounded by these chunks of ice lined in a certain pattern, almost like a premade path. The balance shifted, wobbling the floating object.

"Okay, we need to jump from ice to ice. Be careful not to crack them, or else we'll freeze to death in the cold water!" I warned.

She nodded in response then took the first leap, and just like that, she cleared it effortlessly. I followed in her footsteps, careful not to land in the wrong place. There were a few pieces that felt way too small to be floating amongst the big pieces. Nonetheless, I gave them a shot. On my last leap, I misstepped on a hidden branch, which popped up from the ground, and lost my balance. I fell onto my rear end in a pile of hardened snow. I was completely engulfed by the white powder, covering me from head to toe. The fall threw me for a loop. I placed my hand upon my chest as if I could calm my racing heartbeat. My arms and legs felt tingly, almost completely numb. I guess my body was in shock from the sudden slip of my foot. In that moment, I felt like I was about to die, yet Madeline had to regain composure in order to not laugh. I could see her cheeks puff and turn red from holding back her laughter. Her lips pursed before completely letting go and accepting that she couldn't hold back her cackling any longer. Her arms crossed at her stomach as she leaned forward, emptying her lungs in cheery laughter, at my expense.

"You should have seen your face!" she howled.

I stood up, shaking off the excess snow. I could still see a few stray snowflakes latching onto the loose wool hairs on my sweater. My boots were completely covered in white by the time I pulled myself out of the pile.

"You would have made the same face too…" I sulked.

After that ordeal, we continued on with our adventure. By this time, the dog had run off after hearing Madeline's loud mouth. We gave up on finding Bigfoot, which gave me ample time to show her what we really came for: to pay a visit to my heavenly friend.

I placed my heel against the tree that guided my way to Benji. Madeline watched closely, imitating me. I took my first step, heel to heel. Madeline followed. I took my second step, heel to heel. Madeline did so, also. After the two steps, I assumed she got the jist of it and picked up my pace. Eventually, we made it to the site where my leaden scarf laid. I wasn't sure how to break the news to Madeline. I wasn't even sure if she understood what was going on, but I knew I trusted her enough to show her. I stopped walking and faced her. She picked up on the ominous vibe I was giving off.

"Okay, so… I don't want you to be scared—promise me you won't be scared!" I held up my pinkie.

Without any hesitation, she locked her pinkie with mine, twisting it together with stern connected gazes. I took in a deep breath.

"So, Madeline. I would like you to meet my best friend..." I stepped aside to reveal the gravesite. "His name was Benji, and he was my dog."

I couldn't read her face as accurately as I had hoped. She stared in awe at the site I prepared without a single word or breath leaving her mouth. Suddenly, her eyes widen. I could almost see the fascination form outside of her mind. Her mouth would widen then close as if she thought of a million questions but couldn't combobulate it into a single one.

Eventually, she settled on the reply, "that's so cool..."

At that moment, a car horn honked loudly, shattering the atmosphere. Through the trees, we could see a burgundy van pulled over slightly on the side of the road. Mrs. Bleu came to get Madeline before she could even begin sharing her thoughts with me. We didn't even get to truly talk to Benji the way I did with Annalise. However, I knew that things had to come to an unfortunate end eventually. I walked her back to the main road. Mrs. Bleu still had a cheery smile plastered on her face when we showed up. Before she got in the car, she whipped around and dug into her pockets.

"I almost forgot to give this back to you." She pulled out my Rubik's Cube.

I reached to grab it from her palm but stopped myself.

"You can keep it."

My response took her aback. "Are you sure?"

I nodded.

She smiled and then gave me a warm hug. For the first time since my last meeting with Annalise, I felt cherished and warm. Sure, I was given plenty of hugs by my mother and father, but it felt different this time. She pulled away; although, I wanted to keep the hug as long as I possibly could.

We exchanged our goodbyes as she hopped into the car. She quickly buckled then faced the window as the car pulled away from the side of the road. I kept waving away the van until it was no longer in sight. I would have liked to believe she didn't look away until the very end. Though she was gone, I felt the most content I had ever been.

The trees swayed to hover over me; however, I didn't feel intimidated. The birds sang in celebration, and the clouds uncovered the sun. It felt like nature was finally on my side for once. No—rather, I could feel Benji's acceptance of my new friend. His tail wagged, creating the breeze that shook the branches. I smiled at the fact that Benji liked her. I wouldn't have known what to do if he didn't.

As the breeze grew stronger, I was sure that one day, I'd bring her back to finally meet Benji.

December 13, 1998

Dear Annalise,

Where did you go? I havent seen you in so long. A friend came over today. Her mom did too. She called me hansome. Do you think I am hansome? Anyways I want to see you soon.

Love, Clyde.

※ 102

Chapter Six

Teakettle

BRIGHT AND EARLY, Tuesday mornings had a subtle flare. The fresh dew gathered at the bottom of the windowsill, the iciness painstakingly creeping up on it like a predator to prey. Orange flames ignited the powdered snow, dimming as the clouds swept by. My mother had already set the teakettle on the stovetop. It would cry out to her a few times, but I doubted my mother could hear it from the top floor. She took the radio up to the bedroom for who knows what. I could hear muffled music playing, but it wasn't the happy kind; rather, the songs related more to loneliness than joy. I hopped off the couch and ran over to the stove. Steam blew out from the air hole and spout of the kettle. I stepped up onto the pink plastic stepping stool and held onto the warm handle. Gently, I lifted the pot off of the gate. My small wrist barely had enough strength to keep it above the flame. The water sloshing inside didn't help either. As my wrist shook, I failed to notice my inability to lift it higher. The base of the pot nicked the iron grate, spilling boiling water out of the spout. A bit of it splashed onto my hand, causing me to drop the entire pot. On instinct, I tried to catch it before it hit the floor. I let out a cry as my hand grazed the searing stainless steel of the pot. I stepped off the stepping stool and ran over to the sink. Cold water shot out from the faucet, soothing the burn. I left it in the running water, scared to remove it, while the gas stove still burned brightly. I felt slightly relieved when I heard heavy footsteps pummeling down the staircase. I had never seen my mother so frantic before. She hastily switched off the gas burner, fanning away at the air. She then threw down a plethora of colorful rags on the steaming puddle of tea water. This was all done without the acknowledgement of my presence. She stood with her hands on her hips, peering down at the mess. It wasn't until she heard the running sink water that she looked up.

"Oh, what did you do..." She walked over to inspect the injury.

A red welt formed around the area of my palm and the side of my hand. My mother wrapped a damp paper towel around it and went to fetch a bag of ice. She whipped open drawers and cupboards without any idea in her mind of what to do. I couldn't blame her, though. One second, she was listening to some solid jazz, and in the next, the tea kettle crashed onto the kitchen floor with her freshly boiled water spilled into every crack and crevice in the tiles. She eventually found a plastic bag and filled it to the rim with ice. She zipped it up and placed on the burn. I flinched. My mother patted my back while elevating my hand. She seemed less stressed but had tenseness in her brows. The makeshift ice pack seemed to have worked, and my mother was satisfied with it as was I. Afterwards, I was sent to rest on the couch to return to looking out the living room window. My mother returned up the steps. The closing of the door sounded. Moments later, the music resumed. The dew had somewhat crystallized with a glistening glimmer. The once ignited areas of snow had slowly melted down from their previous size. I peered down at the road that followed to the woods.

 Bright and early, Tuesday mornings had a subtle flare.

106

Chapter Seven

Envy

A BEAD OF SWEAT ran down my father's forehead as he hauled his hefty tools onto the wagon. My mother wanted him to build a new porch since the old wood had soaked up a good decade or two of neglect. I didn't mind how it looked; though, it was a pain tripping over exposed rusty nails in the floorboards. I could see this porch wasn't going to be an easy project by the looks of it. My father had already gone through 10 tall glasses of water and five unfortunate freshly washed hand towels.

While my father worked, I watched idly through the living room window. The snow had melted, but the nippy air remained. Whenever my father looked my way, I'd breath on the glass until it became the perfect slate for drawing. I dragged my finger across the frosted glass, making simple shapes of different sizes. He'd smile at symbols like hearts, snowflakes, and tear drops but raised a brow whenever I wrote actual messages. It never occured to me that the message didn't look the same on the other side of the glass. I began to get frustrated. Each question I wrote on the glass got ignored by a shrug or quick glance. I eventually gave up and receded into the comfy cushions of the couch. The fireplace flickered glowing sparks into the air until they diminished into floating ash. Every crackle and pop made me jolt. The aroma of freshly cut cherry wood and maple loomed throughout the house. I pulled the comforter up to my chin. I guess I had ended up falling asleep on the couch the night before while listening to a few early 1990s classics. Although it was a bit late for the holiday, a few Christmas jams serenaded me to sleep. I felt toasty with *Sleigh Bells* playing in the background. It was much warmer here than in my room.

The jingling of bells sounded. My mother entered through the back door. The hems of her jeans were soaked as were her shoes. She didn't seem to mind them being wet. She swung her coat around the backing of the kitchen chair and slid her shoes off. I didn't know whether or not to greet her. Her eyes, emotionless, only blinked every 10 seconds or so. Her once glowing porcelain skin lacked color. She had no pink in her cheeks—just hints of gray. I didn't get to see her smile nor the two dimples on her cheeks. For the first time, I saw my mother out of her own body. She simply wasn't *her*.

My father opened up the front door. He stood at the entrance with his hand still wrapped around the doorknob. He studied my mother's nerve-racking stance, careful of how to approach her. Her arms crossed her waist with her shoulders perked up high. She felt uncomfortable, and you could read it plainly across her face. She took a quick glance at my father and then sat down. He subsequently removed his boots and slid them into their designated cubby. I receded deeper into the couch cushions. The silence scared me the most. A log slid from the grate, creating a miniature explosion of ash. My father seemed to walk right past it. I couldn't help but watch as if it were a scene from a movie. They sat close together, almost inseparable. He watched her lips move as she mouthed each word. Some words, unfortunately, I couldn't make out. She collapsed into my father's arm, crying, I assumed. He had such a stern look on his face. He hadn't a doubt in his mind of what to do.

I climbed off the couch, bundling the comforter into the crevice of the cushions. Steadily, I made my way over to the kitchen table. My father invited me with open arms. It was tempting, but I hesitated. I was scared. The atmosphere felt different. It felt colder. I didn't like the cold very much.

"Come, Clyde. You're mother could really use some support right now." My father motioned for me to come forward.

I let him wrap his arms around me and my mother, but I wasn't sure who to hug back. In her hand, she held a photo. The color was dull but present. The date stamped in the right corner in yellow read 11/19/1971. There was an older gentleman with a woman. The older gentleman had blond, wavy hair in a peculiar style while the woman wore a bright blue dress with a pearl necklace and feathered hat. Between them, a little girl stood with a bright, toothy smile. It was the same as my mother's. The little girl wore the same shade of red lipstick that she probably stole from her mother's dresser. Her arms were held behind her back with a straightened posture. The entire family seemed happy and content.

My mother set the photo down and placed her finger shakily below the man's face. She gained her composure, opening her mouth to speak.

"This is your grandfather, Clyde. My father." She moved the photo closer to the edge of the table. "He decided this morning that… he wanted to give Benji a visit. He isn't here with me—us, anymore."

I stared at the picture. It was hard to feel *anything*. There was no pain, no grief, and no sadness, but I felt there should have been *something*. My mother was torn, heartbroken, but I wasn't. I had never met my grandfather, and I couldn't feel for a man I never met. I had never felt so lost.

My father read this as a sign to step away from the situation. He lifted me up and carried me to the stairs. My mother didn't react. She didn't even move. Her eyes were glued to the photo. I could read it in the tensing muscles on her face that it meant *something* to her. It held stories only known to those within the picture. It wasn't one of those stories written in words on a colored page; it was one I could never fathom to experience. It was her story.

"Okay, that's enough for today. Why don't you play with your toys in your room until suppertime? I'll be back in a bit. Stay strong for me, Slugger." He patted me on the head and then left the room.

I felt guilty for not being able to comfort my mother; though, I couldn't quite understand what was wrong. All I knew and felt was envy. He got to see Benji, and that was all that mattered to me. Another stranger got to see Benji before I did. It was selfish, but it hurt more than anything. He got to hold him and hug him. He got to see his tail wag and tongue sticking out of his mouth. He was able to play fetch with him again and again for eternity. It was sickening how much I envied him, but it wasn't something I could help nor stop. It was my story.

January 2, 1998

Dear Annalise,

How was your day? Mine was okay. Well it was kinda bad. My grandfather went to visit Benji. My mom is sad about it. Maybe we can meet again and say hi to them. I can tell my mom! Are you coming back to see me? I want to see you again. You can meet my mom. She is really nice! I will talk to you later. Bye for now.

Love, Clyde.

※ 114

Chapter Eight

Amnesia

T̲h̲e̲ ̲s̲h̲e̲e̲t̲s̲ ̲o̲f̲ ̲w̲h̲i̲t̲e̲ gave way to the green of the earth. I began seeing a few birds return from their long vacation in the south; however, the Blue Jays never left Caershire. I watched them come back to the place that once held their nests to find it empty. They'd consult their spouses, bickering whether to stay or to leave. In the end, they fled and never returned. I had always wondered where they ended up.

My mother hadn't yet recovered from the loss of my grandfather. She stayed in the bedroom for most of the day. I wasn't allowed to go up and check on her. My father said it was best to stay downstairs and listen to the radio. I kept the volume down just in case I heard my name being called from the upstairs bedroom. At times, I would jerk my head to the slightest hum or creak when it was really just the house settling in. Desperation can be an evil spirit sometimes.

In between the time of today and when Madeline left, I had written six letters to Annalise. Though, I didn't get any back. I blamed the postal service for not delivering the letters. Although, a part of me relied on the possibility of it being stolen or lost rather than accepting that she didn't acknowledge it entirely. My mother would tell me horror stories of people stealing other people's mail. The world could be cruel sometimes. I had a grudge against Santa for awhile for not returning any letters or giving me the gifts I asked for. My raging fits would be tempered down by my mother's reason of why I didn't get the bright red fire truck I always wanted. She'd say the mailman had to deliver millions of letters, so my letter must have gotten lost. Still, that reason didn't satisfy me. Santa was magical, so my wishes should have been answered. It wasn't until my father broke the devastating news to me that

Santa wasn't *real* when I stopped holding contempt against Christmas day.

My father entered through the back door. He wore a black shirt. No—his shirt was gray. I couldn't remember. He was drenched in sweat from head to toe. He snatched the truck keys from the key ring and looked over to me. He mumbled a few words that I barely have any recollection of. I believe it was something along the lines of needing to run by the store. I nodded in response, and he left.

I watched the blue truck pull away from the driveway, shift gears, then skid as my father slammed on the gas pedal. The truck left a trail of exhaust that eventually blocked my entire view of the road.

I hopped off the couch and headed up the steps only to stop near my bedroom door to listen to my mother. I heard a few sniffles here and there with slight whimpering. She'd weep her father's name and throw in a few of her mother's. I crept toward her bedroom, careful not to make the slightest creak. My father told me not to bother her, but I was raised on support and comfort. My heart ached knowing that behind the wooden door, my mother was hurting. I hesitantly reached for the shiny doorknob. Right when my delicate fingertips met with the brass, it yanked open, showing my mother on the other side. I inhaled sharply, afraid to make any movement. She seemed to be taken back just slightly, but I couldn't tell how she felt through her solemn eyes. They were puffy. I was surprised she could even see with how puffy they were. There were two—NO, three boxes of tissues on the floor. Kleenex tissues I believe. After our first contact with the eyes, she failed to look at me again. Her hands came off the doorknob, and she slid passed me down the steps. She didn't question why I stood at her door. She didn't even say hello. She simply ignored me.

I gnawed on my lower lip. She left me alone on the top floor. My cheeks felt red hot. I felt a bit guilty for not saying anything, but also, a bit embarrassed for being ignored. I fled to my bedroom. I made sure to lock the door behind me after I entered. The guilt ate me up inside. I felt this was my doing somehow. She didn't even want to see me. I hid under the covers, pulling the pillows close to my chest. I wanted to say a million things to my mother to comfort her, but I couldn't get just one word out.

As I fought with myself, a loud thud came from my bedroom window. I paused, scared to make any movement. The thud returned again. I flipped the sheets off and stared at the window. A few seconds passed before a ball of melted ice and snow splattered against the glass. I immediately ran over, ready to scold whoever was trying to shatter my window. Instead, I was greeted by someone else. Someone I longed for for weeks.

Annalise stood down below, waving up at me. In her hand was another snowball, which I questioned where she found the snow to do so since most of it had started melting. Only a few stubborn piles failed to melt all the way.

I pulled the lock and lifted the window. She dropped the snowball then fluttered her fingers in my direction. My lips curled as my cheeks tightened. I smiled so hard I could barely see. I waited so long to see her again that it almost felt like a dream. She giggled, leaning forward, then standing straight up.

"Come down here!" she shouted.

I bobbed my head before backing away from the window. I quickly pulled on my wool socks, threw on a coat, then dashed out of my room. As I went down the stairs, I stumbled on the last step, catching myself on the banister. My boots were laced with the best of my abilities due to me not really knowing how to tie my shoes properly. I whipped open my front door, careful not to slam it behind me. Annalise stood in the grass with her hands held behind her back. Her dimples began to show as she smiled. I hadn't noticed them before.

"Guess what I found," she said, already eager to say.

"What is it?" I replied, also eager to know.

"Come with me." She turned around and headed for the road. "I found it in the woods."

I stopped in my tracks, looking back at the house. My mother was inside, and I wasn't sure if I should leave her. Annalise noticed that I didn't follow suit.

"What is it?" she asked, disappointingly.

I chewed on the insides of my cheek, scared that if I said anything about my mother, Annalise would leave. I shook my head.

"It's nothing..." I said. "I just think... we should take the wagon if we're going there. I'll pull you on it!"

Her eyes lit up. At the time, I didn't consider if I was able to pull another person on the wagon given that the wagon was heavy enough. She ran over to the wagon that sat in the garage. Without wiping it down, she hopped inside. I lifted the handle and began pulling. Luckily, she wasn't that heavy. Pulling the wagon out of the mud was a bit tough but doable.

We made our way to the woods. Annalise didn't say much. I didn't either, but I had hundreds of ideas racing in my mind. I wondered what she found and why it was so important for me to go with her. Maybe she had a present for me and this was her way of surprising me with it. I shook my head. It couldn't be.

"Right here!" she shouted.

We parked the wagon and left it on the side of the road. She didn't even wait for me before running off into the woods. I trailed behind her, wondering what adventures lay ahead of me.

Eventually, she stopped under one of the dogwood trees, pointing up at the top. Hanging on one of the branches was a paper airplane. It fluttered as the wind blew but was still stuck between the branches. I looked over at Annalise.

Her eyes glossed over as she looked over at me. She didn't have to say words for me to know how much she cherished that paper airplane. Her hands were clenched up and held up to her chin. Her puppy-dog eyes enchanted me. It was like a spell. I couldn't say no.

I placed my hand against the trunk of the tree. The paper airplane seemed so high up. It called my name over and over again, taunting me. I jammed my foot into a small crevice of the tree then pulled myself with a higher branch. The paper airplane looked miles away from me. I held on tightly to the branch, depending on it with my life. Annalise gleamed with pride and joy. She cheered me on silently. I took this as a push to keep going. I reached for the next branch and placed my foot higher than its previous position. As I climbed, the wind grew stronger. I kept going, reaching for one branch after another. The higher I got, weirdly, the more confidence I felt.

"You're almost there! You're doing amazing!" she cheered.

I smirked, knowing that I'd be a hero in her eyes after I got the paper airplane. It was so close to me. In fact, it would have only taken one last branch up before I got it. I stepped upon the next branch, ready to use it to push myself up to grab the paper airplane above me. Without a doubt, the plane could have been in my hands my now. Annalise would have been happy. She'd generously hug me if I got it. As I bared my weight on the limb, it snapped. The paper just barely touched my finger tips. I wailed my arms in the air, desperate to grab something, anything. In the next moment, the world flashed nothingness. I forced my eyelids open for a mere second, catching a glimpse of white dust falling from the sky above.

Then, the nothingness returned.

Chapter Nine

Temporary

"*Clyde.*"

My eyes fluttered open.

I caught a glimpse of the flashing car lights. A hand caressed my face. I laid my head upon my mother's lap. I heard muffled yelling. My parents were arguing about who knows what. I was in the truck without any recollection of how I got there. Though, I didn't say a word.

I closed my eyes.

"—*New Jersey.*"

I opened my eyes.

My father must have slammed on the breaks. My mother's hand jutted out to stop us from crashing into the car seats. Her other hand gripped my arm. He hopped out of the truck and shut the car door behind him.

I closed my eyes again.

"*Help!*"

My eyelids were forced open. A bright light was shined into them. I squinted. Above me, rectangle-shaped lights passed by us, flashing on and off. I heard the squeaking of wheels beneath me.

"Stay awake, Sweetie. Can you do that?" The lady beside me asked.

"*Mhm…*" I mumbled in reply.

The double doors burst open. I was greeted with many people dressed in white. They didn't have the friendliest faces. I saw on the reflection of a metal pole my parent peeking through a square glass window.

I can't remember what happened much after that.

Chapter Ten

If you could be mine

I STARED AT THE WOODEN DESK, aimlessly. I couldn't form a single thought about it. I couldn't conceive anything about how the wood was splitting at the legs, how the paint had chipped from my chair rubbing against it, or how cluttered the papers lying on top of it appeared. I couldn't come up with one single thought. My mind was in a total fog.

The walls in my house weren't thick enough. I really wished they were. Behind the dandelion-colored wallpaper, the muffled shouting of my parents resounded through every crack and crevice until all I could hear was them bickering. However, at that moment, I felt nothing. My head throbbed, killing every thought that could have occured. Everything that I heard in one ear went out the next along with everything I saw and felt. My mind floated in a river bed of confusion, riding along the streams. The pounding headaches were an annoyance. I wanted to be outside with Annalise or visit downtown again. I wanted to tease Madeline for her toothless smile and talk to Benji, but the universe forbade me to do so.

My parents continued their bickering. Their voice levels fluctuated between shouting and mere whispers. Their attempts at lowering their voice so I couldn't hear them were pointless. I heard every word they said.

In a daze, I slid off the bed, shoving the bedsheets aside. I shuffled my way through the littered floor and crouched down at the wall. I pressed one ear against it, covering the other with my hand.

"I left for half an hour, Claire. How could you let him out alone like that?" I assumed my father said.

"I didn't know he left, Tom. I can't watch him 24/7. It's a difficult time for me right now," my mother replied.

"Did you see the stitches on his head? This is the second time he left without you knowing," he reminded my mother.

I lifted my hand and gently touched the back of my head. My fingers lightly ran over a rough spot, which I assumed were the stitches.

"There's just so much going on in my life, and you're leaving..." she wept.

There was a pause. My mother sniffled here and there. She'd inhale sharply and sigh. A throbbing sensation erupted within my head. I pressed my forehead against the drywall as hard as I could. I was ready to pull away to lie down again when my mother began to mumble a few words. None of them caught my attention until she raised her voice.

"Please take him, Tom. Take him with you. I can't do this anymore!"

I pulled away sharply, taken aback by her comment. *Take him.* She didn't want me anymore? *Take him with you.* What if I didn't want to go? *Take him.* I didn't want to leave. *I don't love him anymore.* It repeatedly stabbed my heart.

I scurried under my covers. My head floated upon my shoulders with my throat burning with rage. The thought that she didn't want me anymore replayed in my mind. I thrashed the pillows with my balled up fists until they were no longer cloud-like and fluffy. I hated them. I hated everything in this room. I slung the pillows around, knocking over a few knickknacks. Up next were the covers and then the sheets. I swiped my arms across my desk until all of the contents spilled onto the floor.

"Clyde!" My parents burst through the door.

I was swept up by my father and placed on the bed. My mother stood in shock, shifting her eyes around the room. She attempted to take everything in at once, but the mess became too much for her.

"What is going on with you, Clyde? You're making this very difficult for us!" she snapped.

I hopped off my father's lap and stood in front of her with my arms locked beside me. The steam could be seen fuming from the top of my head if you looked closely enough.

"You said you didn't want me anymore!" I shouted. "You told Daddy to take me away! What if I don't want to leave? Why can't I say something?"

Mother bit her tongue, her eyes watering as I ranted.

"I don't want to leave because... because Mrs. Bleu thinks I'm handsome—you heard her say it—and it wouldn't be nice to take me away... and I'm supposed to beat Madeline in an arcade game, and Benji is still here, and I like Annalise very much, but I can't love someone when I'm in New Jersey!" I sobbed.

"Love? What is this about love, Sweetie? Who's Annalise?" my father asked.

"She doesn't matter anymore because I'll be gone and you want me gone!" I exploded.

"I need you to calm down, Clyde. You're getting worked up." My mother raised her hands.

"I don't want to calm down! I want to stay here!" I yelled back at her.

I picked up the closest action figure and shot it across the room, the arms breaking off the body as it smashed against the wall. There was a golf ball-sized dent where it hit. The unfortunate toy laid lifeless on the floor.

"That's it!" Mom yanked me closer, jabbing her finger into my chest. "You are old enough to know that not everything is as bright and shiny as you think it is. I need you to really grow up, Clyde. I mean it!"

She turned her face, relieving the burning sensation behind her nose as tears welled up in her eyes.

"If you were mine, you wouldn't be like this," she faintly vowed.

My throat tightened up. Although my ears were wide and usually welcoming, they didn't expect to hear what was said. No one was.

"Claire, that's enough..." my father growled.

She let go of my arm, turning her back on me and marching away. Her words punched me in the gut mercilessly .

I thought that everything I spewed would have persuaded her to keep me. I believed that I had some leverage in this fight. I thought I won the argument and that the reward was to stay home with everyone who had built this town from the ground up and things would never change. I really thought I had made a dent.

"Your mother is just upset. Don't mind what she says. She doesn't mean it, I'm sure," my father tried to comfort me.

I took a step back. It felt like the odds were against me.

"I don't have to go to New Jersey until the end of this month. That's plenty of time for you to say goodbye to your friends." He patted my back. "Listen, I used to be in your shoes. I didn't want to move from my hometown either."

There was no acknowledgement of what was said. He avoided it at all cost. He darted his eyes away as soon as my eyes met his. I wanted an explanation, an answer, an apology. I wanted something, but I got nothing from him.

Still in my utmost confused mindset, I was moved toward the bed. We sat down together on the sheetless mattress. His head lowered as did mine.

"I moved here 20 years ago at the same age of eight. Imagine," he shifted his seating position, "an eight-year-old boy moving from my childhood home to an entirely new place with the expectation that I had to start over and be fine with it all. It was... terrifying."

He took a second to gather his thoughts as if he felt that he was losing my interest.

"But, there's some good to the story. If I didn't move, I wouldn't have met your mother." He paused. "And if I didn't meet your mother, you... wouldn't be here today. You just have to find the good in things."

Dad rested his hand on my shoulder.

"You know what my pops and I did before I left my hometown?" He waited until I looked up. "We took a few old boxes and some photos and made ourselves a time capsule."

"A time capsule?" I echoed.

"Oh yes, a time capsule. It had bright blue paint on it with stars, and it resembled a time machine almost! It held so many precious memories like my baby pictures, drawings, toys, and many other things. It's a part of me that never had to leave the town."

I was caught in awe over this idea. In my mind, I had already formulated a game plan on how I was going to tackle this project. I wanted clouds on my box with stars. I wanted the sun shining high up in the sky and birds flying. In the box, I wanted my letters inside of it, every letter I had sent to Annalise. I wanted the capsule to be protected by this town so nothing could get to them. I planned to plant the time capsule directly under the dogwood tree. Anyone who would try to steal it would have to go through the pits of lava and giant grizzly monsters before they got to my box.

"Let's use this box." My father lifted the velvet blue box. "It's the perfect size."

It was way too small. I couldn't fit every valuable object I dreamed of inside the tiny box. I needed a whole packing container for the amount of stuff I had.

My face scrunched. I shook my head and said, "too small."

"Too small? No, of course not. It's the perfect size." He crouched down. "If you put everything you ever wanted to keep inside this box, they would all be just bland—ordinary. That's why you have to pick the most valuable items to stash inside of it so the feeling of opening it again will be much more rewarding, okay?"

I nodded.

I was limited in my options. What could I possibly fit into that tiny box which still held meaning to it? I glanced around the room. My army men would take up too much space. I didn't really find them that special anyway. Marvin couldn't fit inside, nor could my rocket ship nor sailboat. The unsent letters wouldn't all fit, so I needed to choose the most special one. I gave Madeline my Rubik's Cube, so there went that option. I was stuck on what I should choose.

"I'll give you time to think about it." Dad placed the box back on the nightstand.

Before he left, he reached down to pick up my coat, which was lying on the ground. As the coat was lifted, clanking came from the pockets. My father raised a brow as he held it, wondering what mischievous things I kept inside it. I dug my arm inside of the left pocket and pulled out two or three golden tokens from the arcade downtown. Suddenly, I remembered the bet I made with Madeline. I officially decided that this was going to be an item added to the box just in case the time came when I needed a token or two.

My father left the room shortly after. I assumed it was to calm down my mother. Through the little talk I had with my dad, I had already forgotten about the ordeal. The guilt began to set in. I snapped so hard at my own mother, but at the same time, it felt justified. Was I really too much to handle? I didn't think much of my behavior. In fact, every memory that came to my mind was good rather than nasty ones. Where did things go wrong?

I heard footsteps coming from the hallway. They trampled down the steps and onto the bottom floor with a loud click of the heels. I listened as someone grabbed the keys off the keyring and slammed the back door. I looked through the window to see my mother getting inside the truck. The congested engine roared as the key twisted in the ignition. I heard the tires squeal as she slammed the gear into reverse. The exhaust polluted the air as she drove off to who knows where. My head began to pound again as my heart sank to my stomach. I quickly fitted the sheets onto the mattress and threw the covers and pillows back onto the bed. I slipped under the chilled blankets and pulled it over my head. My father's words resonated in my ears: *you just have to find the good in things*. I'd be lying if I said I didn't try. I couldn't find the goodness in my mother's sudden hatred toward me. Her words alone sucked all of the goodness out of the room. Solitude, disgust, and disappointment were all that was left inside this room after her words. It was suffocating. Through a tiny crack between the walled up blankets, I could see a clear view of the sapphire blue velvet box. My father was right. All of my toys weren't worthy enough to be put inside and protected by the woods. I had to choose carefully.

 I rested my eyes. As the darkness consumed the entire bedroom, I began to imagine what New Jersey would look like. My father brought back a few postcards with images of the cities. First, I saw tall skyscrapers, which barely touched the clouds and planes that soared through the sky. The roads held so many cars. I couldn't imagine driving in such a congested place. I had hoped to earn my license in this small town of Caershire, but now, I was faced with the possibility of actually driving in the chaos. The city was met with greenish-blue waters. They rippled slightly from the wind. It was astonishing how close the city was to the ocean. It gave me a bit of anxiety just thinking about it. Finally, I imagined my father and me arriving in New Jersey, seeing the skyscrapers hovering over us the farther we drove in. Some jazz music played on the car radio as the scenery reflected off the glass of our windows. Nevertheless, I imagined a brand new beginning to the start of my life, a new life aware from my hometown of Caershire, Pennsylvania.

Chapter Eleven

Time Capsule

THE BLUE VELVET PEEKED THROUGH my inner coat pocket with an obvious box shaped outline. As I marched on the pavement, the golden arcade tokens clinked together. It weighed the left side of my coat down, slugging around as I walked. The road was slick and wet from the previous night's storm. My father held my hand to ensure I wouldn't trip or wobble off the road. The concussion symptoms began to depart days before, but the headaches lingered. I didn't mind them as much now.

Over the past few days, I had been on autopilot. I hadn't stepped out of my room except to use the bathroom and maybe snatch a quick snack from the kitchen. I spent most of my bedridden days recovering alone in my room. My father had brought in the stereo and switched to the latest NPR station to keep my mind busy. The *pitter-patter* of rain would pummel the roof tiles as the anchorman presented the weekly news updates, and strikes of lightning would illuminate my room when the sun fell below the horizon.

I looked back to the window where the candle wick remained unlit. It had been like that for days. My father was the only other person to step foot inside my room since the incident with my mom besides myself. I hadn't seen my mother since she had left. I would ask my father of her whereabouts, but the question would be dodged by the comment of some random object being *neat* or the weather. I stopped trying after a while.

I took out the sapphire box and shook it near my ear. The coins jangling inside the box were music to my ears. The flattened draft of a potential letter rested at the bottom, muffling the noisiness of the coins. I added a few stickers inside and a cut piece of Benji's leash. Although my mother and I had a fallout, I wanted to keep my cherished memories with her too. I stole the bookmark out of her book and kept it inside the box. We had made it together. The bookmark was created by folding a strip of paper into a heart and inscribing *C.W* at the top since our initials were the same. It wasn't anything spectacular, but I remember doing it together. I also kept a memory of my father's. I took a printed photo of my father's side of the family with me in the middle and placed it inside. We took it the day my father purchased the land. I remember the fiery ambition that burned brightly within his soul with that simple plot of land. He wanted to build my mother a second house with a pond full of fish, but when the price came around, his dreams were crushed. She didn't expect much of it anyway. It was deemed too ambitious.

"What's inside?" My father asked. "Or is it a secret?"

I thought about it for a second.

"You'll find out later," I replied, grinning from ear to ear.

I wanted him to feel the same as I would when I opened it 10, 20, 30 years from now. I hoped to return back to this very house and these woods and open the box on our front porch with my parents sitting beside me. The tarnished latch would probably fail to open at the first attempt. It would take a dampened wash cloth to clean the grime off in order for the latch to unlock smoothly. Inside, the photos would be untouched, as if they remained frozen in time. The golden tokens would reflect the sunlight as I took them out to inspect the intricate details inscribed in the gilded brass, and at the very bottom, still undisturbed from their slumber, the smoothly folded unsent letters to Annalise lay. I imagined tears, maybe, coming from my mother. My father would have an uncrackable smile stretched across his face, and I would be in my own world, a whole other world of what ifs.

We arrived at the opening in the woods. After the snow melted, my father gathered various branches and stuck them together to make an arch to walk under as we entered his land. Any simpleton could just walk around it, but it's never the same as walking through the portal to another realm. Of course, that piece was a new renovation to his land. I think it made the transition easier, almost effortless. My father and I walked under the arch and into the woods. He had to crouch a bit to avoid a misfortunate run in with a couple of loose twigs and branches. I was the perfect height, maybe even a little bit too perfect. I had an easy foot or two of clearance.

Before my father wandered off into the vast area of the woods, I pulled him toward the dogwood tree. I couldn't possibly bury my box under just any tree or in any soil. The area held the memories of my first tether ball before the ball popped off the string, the memories of my first swing set before the thin wood split after sitting in the rain for days, the resting area for my best friend, and the place where I met my beloved

Annalise. It would be sacrilegious of me to bury it anywhere else.

"The roots will be a little tough to dig around. Are you sure you want it here?" my father questioned.

To which I satisfactorily replied, "Yes."

The lined tip of the shovel jammed straight into the earth, ripping out sections of dirt and roots. A few pebbles would clink against the steel blade. Repeatedly, he dug deeper and deeper, hitting different colored layers of soil. It lightened, then darkened, then reddened, then browned. A few living creatures, such as worms and rolleypolleys, snuck into the sections of dirt that were unfortunately scooped away by my father. After a good foot or two was dug, my father stepped aside so I could place the box into the hole.

"Wait!" He dug inside his pockets and pulled out two grocery bags from our local grocery store. "Wrap this around it so the velvet will stay nice."

I double-bagged the box and tied it off with twine and then placed it gently upon the freshly dug soil. I stayed low, afraid to let go of the box. I had a nagging feeling something was missing from the stash of memories. My father's impatient foot tapping caused me to step away, immediately regretting my choices. He scooped the dirt right on top of the box. There was no turning back after this. The dirt landed in the hole with a soft thud. Toward the end, I was reminded by the fact that leaving my hometown was definitely going to happen. Inside that box was the only piece of me that the town had left. I tried to shake off the desolate empty feelings, but they latched on and wouldn't let go.

The back of the shovel slammed against the flattened soil. I noticed lines of sweat running down his face. The air, although chilly, felt pretty dense. It became harder to breath, becoming somewhat similar to thick, condensed fog. This was an obstacle to our agenda, so we weren't able to do much in this weather.

"Alright, that's done. Let's head back." My father dusted his hands off on his pants.

As we walked back to the main road, I found it quite troubling to look away. My eyes were locked onto the burial site, entrusting my father to guide me out of the woods. The more trees we passed, the harder it was to see a full view. I didn't want it to come to an end, but it was inevitable. I glanced around my surroundings. The trees were full of life again, swaying as the wind sang their soulful tunes. The birds found their homes after their long vacations. With the rain, the woods smelled and felt revitalized. I knew I could trust this place.

We reached the arch entrance. Before I went under, I closed my eyes and waited until the winds calmed and the trees were at a standstill. *Please protect my precious velvet box with your life,*

I prayed to myself. My father tugged on my arm. I obliged and followed him under the arch, waving goodbye to the buried box as I left. I vowed to return decades later to that very tree and that, with shovel in hand, I would uncover the eight everlasting years buried under the blooming dogwood tree.

144

Chapter Twelve

Revelation

My mother returned on Thursday, January 18, 1996. In her hand, she held the handle of the baby blue luggage with golden clasps. Her skin seemed to glow much brighter than before as so did her golden locks. I watched her place the house key on the ring behind the banister. She didn't seem as upset as before. In fact, I was certain I saw her lips curl into a smile for a split second before she entered the house.

My father ran down the steps behind me. He stood awkwardly in the living room until my mother noticed him through the kitchen doorframe. He bowed his head. The vestige of her smile faded. She pursed her lips, looking away. I crept out from the staircase and stood beside my father, locking my hand with his.

"Mom…?" I managed to mutter.

Her head spun around in our direction. As she deeply inhaled, her chest protruded then settled as she exhaled. She bit down on her tongue as she pushed her hair behind her ear.

"Hi, Sweetie…" her rosy lips mouthed with a soft voice.

I let go of my father's hand and approached her. She opened her arms wide, visibly shaking. I allowed myself to embrace her. Being in her arms felt so warm, but it didn't feel the same as before. Her hugs weren't as firm. She didn't seem to know where to place her arms, and it just felt awkward. I squeezed her tighter, not wanting to let go. Her trembling was apparent even during the embrace. I heard a few soft sniffles before she pushed me away and ran into my father's arms. She collapsed into full sobs, covering her mouth with her hand.

I grasped my clammy hands together, struggling to figure out what to do with them. My father's eyes constantly flipped between my mother and me. He kept his hands around her back, drawing her close, but with me, I had no one. I chewed at the skin of bottom lip, alternating the pressure between my left foot and my right. Eventually, I came to the conclusion that I was officially not wanted there anymore.

I fled up the stairs with my father calling after me. The door slammed behind me as I quickly entered. I locked it and placed my wooden chair strategically under the doorknob. I could hear the pummeling of footsteps coming up to my bedroom. My father's powerful fist banged against the wood.

"Clyde, come out, please," he begged.

I ran over to my window, unlocking the latch and opening it. I had access to the rooftop where I could crawl over to the nearest ladder leaning against the house on the far right. I would run away, never to be seen again. Maybe I'd see Annalise along the way, and she'd come along with me.

The doorknob jiggled viciously with a few more loud knocks following it. I whipped out one of the geography textbooks and found the map of the U.S. I tore it from top to bottom and stashed it inside my bookbag. I opened my drawer and took a few toys for entertainment along the way. I had a few uneaten crackers on my nightstand left over from the night before. I rolled up the opened wrapper and stuffed the snack deep inside the pockets of my bag. Lastly, I pulled a sticky note from my school desk and scribbled the words Good Bye in red pen.

My father sighed. He jiggled the doorknob slightly then knocked once more.

I swung the bag onto my back and hurried over to the windowsill, swinging my leg over the ledge. I found it troubling to move from this position. It felt like this was a sudden life or death decision, so I had to choose my answer carefully. I was stuck between two realms, forced to pick the one which was the better path. I looked back at the wooden door, hearing only silence from the other side. They must have already given up on me. I lowered my head and clenched the frame of the window. My skin dug into the crevices of the splintered wood. My other leg slowly began to follow.

"You're a little too young to understand this, Clyde, and I don't expect much from it, but you remember the picture I gave you when you were seven? The one with all of us in it. We sat under the dogwood tree and watched the clouds through the branches, and you asked me how I felt about buying the land. I replied grateful—thankful, blessed. And then you asked me why." My father paused. "When I was your age, I had just moved to this town from Arizona. My sister and I hated the town at first. We'd insult every aspect of Caershire. It was too small, too quiet, too lonely. We'd comment on how the buildings looked old and rundown, how the streets had weeds growing in every crack in the roads, how the rain wouldn't stop pouring for a whole two weeks, and how people were just too friendly to us. But, no matter what, we couldn't comment on the dogwood trees."

I stopped in my tracks, listening intently to every word. Eventually, I slipped the bag off my shoulder and let it sink into the pillow below me.

"My sister loved the dogwood trees. The way the whites of the flowers bloomed after their green buds appeared. She loved the smell of them and how the petals on the ground reminded her of snowfall. We didn't have much snowfall in Arizona." He sniffed. "Man, she loved those trees…"

A photo slid under the crack of the door. The image was flipped upside down, yet I was still drawn to it. It called my name and wouldn't stop until I looked. I leaned inside, swinging my leg back over the ledge. For a few seconds, I just stared at the photo, hesitant to approach it. I ambled over, crouching down at the door. The photo stuck halfway inside the room, the other half in the hallway. My small fingers pinched the corner of the photo and slid it away from the opening. I lifted it up to meet my eyeline. The picture showed a woman and a child. The child was a newborn. He had very little to no hair on his head, yet the woman, who I assumed was his mother, had lots of it. Her hair was somewhat wavy and ash brown like my father's and mine. I gathered a bunch of my hair and moved it in front of my eyes to compare the color.

"Her name is Anna Whittaker. She's my sister." His voice trembled. "And that little boy was given the name Clyde. She—uh... she didn't exactly have things figured out back then. At the same time, your mother and I were trying to have a child ourselves, but things weren't... working out for us either."

I couldn't detach my focus from the photo. This delicate piece of paper unlocked the answers I'd been searching for my entire life, and even so, I wasn't sure how to handle it. My skin crawled. Had I lived my life with strangers? It was like I didn't know them. I pinched the skin on my arms, hugging myself and stepping further away from the door. If this was a sign to leave, it screamed out loud and clear. I scooped my bookbag off of the floor and threw it on my back. My palms flattened against the ledge. The gentle golden flames kissed my fingertips as the skies transformed into the colors of chrysanthemums. My eyes ran across the narrow stretch of black upon the thawing earth. Beyond the hill, the woods, and Caershire, I wondered what I would find. I wondered if there would be life for me after I hopped over the ledge and climbed down the side of the house—after I waved my burnt sienna house goodbye. Then, I asked myself, did I really want this?

I glanced over my shoulder to the bedroom door. The paint had chipped off the frame. In blue sharpie, short lines marked my height in the previous months. It had been awhile since I measured my height. I was sure I had grown at least an inch or more.

My father's hand slid against the door, pulling away slightly to hit against the wood in a soft knock.

"Clyde, you are still our son, and we love you. You can say 100 times over that you aren't, but God, you are my son. I raised you as such, and that will never change... no matter how fast the world is moving around you, no matter how many people come in and out of your life, no matter what situations you get yourself into, I will always be there for you. Change is inevitable. That's a fact. We can't avoid it, and I'm sure you wish you could. I'm sure you wish you could stay here, and that we could be in the kitchen again, dancing to *The Temptations*. I wish it, too, Buddy, but we can't." He paused. "I'm begging that you listen and hear my words because I love you, Clyde. The only thing that will change between us is us growing stronger together as time goes on. So, please, Clyde, open the d-"

I swung the door wide open. My father held his breath. By now, the tears in my eyes had welled up to the point that a single blink could flood the room. Sure, I wanted to run away. I wanted to flee with Annalise, but I couldn't. In good conscience, I couldn't leave now. It wasn't because I thought my family hated me. It was because Tom and Claire were the only family members I had left. He was right. They had raised me from birth, and I didn't doubt for a second that they were my parents.

Without speaking a single word, we fell into each other's arms. Our embrace tightened until it was almost suffocating. I wanted him to know that I wouldn't leave him because of everything he had done for me, which, in my honest opinion, needed no voice. I gripped the back of his shirt like my life depended on it. If we were on the edge of the world, I wouldn't let go for even a second. I looked down at the picture on the floor and tried to confirm that the bond built from day one between the man I was hugging and me was real. The moment my eyes fell on the woman in the photo, I felt absolutely nothing for her. Through this, I knew that I, Clyde Whittaker, was truly the son of Tom Whittaker and Claire Whittaker.

Chapter Thirteen

Goodbye

My luggage, along with my father's, pressed up against the wall. One held my hand-me-down clothes while the others held my toys and schoolwork. I double checked my room, the kitchen, and the living room to make sure I didn't leave anything behind. I even checked the bathroom to see if I had left any hidden toys in the cracks and crevices. There was no trace of our family ever living in the house we left behind. I also took a few things from home whether or not they were mine. I took a blanket for the road and one or two pillows that had the cute flower patterns on them. They were my mother's pillows that she let me sleep with at night when I was a baby. I hoped she didn't mind me taking them.

"Claire, we're about to take our leave," my father announced.

My mother came down the steps. She stood before us, somewhat nervous. The color had drained from her face, but it still held that shimmering glow. In her hands was a box wrapped in brown paper. She swallowed hard then looked down at the gift.

"The mailman complained about the letters you've been sending, Clyde." She handed me the box. "I hope that you will still remember me when you're in New Jersey."

I accepted the box from her, holding it in my hands. She anxiously rocked back and forth on her heels. I knew she wanted me to open it in front of her. I untied the twine, letting it fall to the floor. Then, I separated the tape from the paper and tore it sideways, slowly revealing the present. The wrappings uncovered a box of red envelopes, the fancy kind that you find at high end boutiques and department stores. Along with it, postal stamps, which depicted a ruffed grouse amidst a bushel of mountain laurels, were taped onto the box of envelopes. The address of our house was written on a sticky note and tacked beside the stamps.

Even if I tried to hold it back, I couldn't help but smile. I could finally write and send Annalise a proper letter. I looked up at my mother, who still had a worried look on her face. I placed the gift on top of my belongings and went in for a hug. She embraced me with no hesitation. The hug felt right this time. It was warm and caring. It didn't feel uncomfortable at all. We pulled away, accepting our limited time together.

"I think it's time for us to leave." My father bowed his head and said, "Goodbye, Claire."

They hugged goodbye, my father patting her on her back as if they were acquaintances rather than husband and wife. They pulled away after not even half a minute of embracing each other.

"I'll call you when we get to New Jersey," my father said.

My mother bit her lower lip and nodded. "Okay."

My father opened the front door and stepped onto the doormat. I popped up the handle on my suitcase and rolled it outside. Mother joined us as we loaded our belongings into the back seat of the truck. She even helped me with my bookbag, placing it in the front since my toys and books were in that bag. The gift was tucked neatly behind my bags. My shoes were placed in a Ziploc and put in the trunk along with my father's shoes. The trunk held some of our bulkier possessions.

We hopped inside the truck, shutting the door beside us. I cranked the window down so I could have a clear view of the house before we left. My mother gave me one last side hug through the window and kissed my forehead lightly. She waved goodbye to my father and flashed a promising smile with hints of desperation. He smiled back at her. The key was jammed into the ignition and twisted until the engine roared to life.

"Bye, Mommy…" I said. "I'll send you a letter as soon as I get home."

She chuckled. "I'll be waiting, then."

My father began to pull away from the driveway. My mother waved goodbye as we reversed out onto the street. My father whipped the car to be parallel with the house before shifting the gear to drive. I waved back at my mother as the truck began to move forward. My mother continued waving goodbye as we drove off. I watched her in the side mirror. I saw the burnt sienna-colored house fade away in the truck's exhaust. We passed by my father's plot of land, catching a glimpse of the dogwood tree, which laid bare of any petals. I waved goodbye to it. Through the gust of wind, which swept by, shaking the limbs, I felt it wave goodbye to me, too.

Chapter Fourteen

Yellow Mittens

We parked our truck in the slanted parking spaces alongside the sidewalk. A few casual strollers ambled across the grocery store entrance. It was drizzling outside. Those walking carried heavy umbrellas with all different shades of the rainbow. A few didn't carry anything. I opened the truck door gently since in my earlier days, I hadn't been very kind to my father's truck. Below me, a large puddle rested in the neglected pothole in the street. I hopped over it, careful not to get my boots wet. I shut the door and walked alongside my father. He pulled me close as we went through the grocery story entrance. We were greeted with cheesy elevator music and the sweet smell of strawberries. The cashiers gave us a welcoming smile as we entered. The rustling of brown paper bags harmonized with the music. My father directed me toward the candy section. The aisle smelled like nothing more than guilt and bribery. The suckers weren't as glossy and irresistible as they used to be. The jawbreakers made my jaws ache rather than tempt me. Nothing looked appetizing.

"Pick anything you want," my father offered.

I shrugged at first. The only thing that caught my eye was the packet labeled "Fun Dip." I pointed toward the candy's direction. My father snatched one or two of them in Cherry Yum Diddly Dip and RazzApple Magic Dip. I wasn't sure what it was because I never had it before. It sure wouldn't hurt to try.

We headed toward the snacks, searching for a few bags of chips we could sneak into our meals for the next few days. My father lifted a grocery basket from the stands and handed it to me. We began stuffing it with original ruffled chips, weird shaped triangle chips, packaged chocolate chip cookies, and goldfish snacks. The basket had gotten too heavy for me to lift off the floor, so my father offered to help. We made our way to the back side of the grocery store after filling our basket with an unnecessary amount of junk food.

"Wait for me out here. I'll be right back." My father dropped the basket beside me. "Don't go anywhere, Clyde."

He slipped inside the door labeled "Male", which I assumed was the bathroom. I patiently leaned on my heels and pressed my back against the wall, watching shoppers pass by. A rather large woman stared as her squeaky cart and grazed the rubber soles of my boots. I kept eye contact with her as if it was a game. She eventually switched her attention to the array of cheeses displayed beside me. I shrugged it off.

"*Psst... Clyde,*" a gentle voice arose.

I looked over to find the source. I would have recognized that hushed voice from a mile away. Annalise hid behind the lone shelf of donuts and other pastries. Her timid demeanor enchanted me. I inched toward her. She giggled, flashing her dazzling smile, then fled as soon as I came within a few feet of her. I followed her into the next aisle. She'd turn around in a taunting manner, giggling as she ran. She paused for a moment, allowing me to catch up. I scuttled over, laughing along like it was a fun game of tag. She sharply turned the corner, weaving into the next aisle in this game of cat and mouse. I continued chasing after her. Her laughter echoed from ear to ear until that's all I could hear. It didn't feel like a game anymore. She taunted me as I followed after her. I huffed as I tried to keep up. My coat became an inconvenience. A wave of coolness flushed through my system. I wanted to tell her I was leaving and that this might be the last time I would see her, but she seemed too caught up in her game that she didn't stop to even say a simple hello. She turned the corner right when I was about to reach her. I tailed her, whipping into the next aisle, screeching to a stop after seeing Annalise stand before me. She didn't flee this time. She just innocently smiled while I was out of breath, panting.

"Morning, Whittaker," she greeted.

"Morning, Miss…Lynn?" I peered down at her coat to confirm.

She chuckled at my attempt to greet her in the same manner.

"Fancy seeing you here again. What brings you here so early in the morning?" she asked.

I opened my mouth to speak but chickened out. I turned my face away, avoiding eye contact of any sorts.

"Hm?" She bent down, making sure she was being seen. "Cat got your tongue, Whittaker?"

I shook my head.

"Well, I saw you outside with your dad a couple of days ago. What were you burying? It seemed important," she asked.

I didn't know what to say. It was hard enough saying hi to her. Breaking the news that I might never see her again seemed a heartbreaking way to start a conversation with her.

"How much did you miss me…?" I managed to mutter.

She was taken aback by the sudden question. Her brows rose as she pondered it. I'm not going to lie, the amount of time she took to come up with an answer kinda hurt my feelings. I thought it was an easy question.

Instead of answering it in words, she opened her arms wide. I mistakenly took it as an invitation for a hug and went in for it. Before I could wrap my arms around her, she pushed me away.

"No! I missed you this much!" She opened her arms up wide again.

I finally understood what she was trying to convey, smiling at her answer. Satisfied that she even missed me, my body tensed as I tried to remove myself from the situation, feeling somewhat flustered. I couldn't wipe the smile off my face for even a second. As if my heart rate wasn't beating fast enough already, it felt 10 times stronger.

The smile faded once I remember the true intentions of the question. In all honesty, I didn't even want to ask another question pertaining to the subject of me moving. She seemed content with how things were going, too.

"What's wrong? You seem upset."

I snapped back into focus, purposefully changing my expression to something less obvious. I twiddled my thumbs. Maybe I could have just ended it with a hug and come up with an alibi of why I couldn't play outside anymore. I could have just told her the wicked witch, Gretal Grindal, cursed me to forever stay inside and that the only way I could talk to her was through written letters. I could have said that I was suddenly diagnosed with an allergy to the sun and that I couldn't go outside, or maybe I was a ghost who couldn't be seen or heard, but I was still able to write her letters. I could have said any of those.

"Would you miss me if... I never saw you again?" I painstakingly asked.

"Of course, I would. What kind of question is that?" Her brows furrowed.

"Oh, well..." I looked around for some sort of cue for me to get out of there. "I... uh... I'm not—Well, I am... moving."

She didn't seem to understand at first. I didn't blame her. I didn't quite announce the news in the most fluent way possible. It didn't take long for the joy to drain from her face. Her shoulders slumped as did the rest of her body. She wouldn't meet my gaze, letting her hair fall forward.

"My dad got a job in New Jersey, and I'm supposed to go with him. I was burying a time capsule in the woods so that in

20 or more years, I can open it again and remember stuff," I told her.

She puffed her chest then immediately dug her hands straight into her pockets. She flipped her right pocket inside out, finding it empty and then worked with her left pocket, pulling out the yellow mittens with the tiny flower embroidered on the rim.

"Take this." She placed it in my hands. "If you're really leaving me, Clyde Whittaker, I want you to remember me forever. Put it in the time capsule so you'll never forget about me. If we don't see each other when we're older, I want you to have a piece of me left with you, okay?"

I panicked. I wasn't sure what to do. She seemed set on the idea of giving me her signature yellow mittens, but I felt that having them was a big enough responsibility.

"I—I can't take these. You keep them. They're yours!" I thrust them back into her hands.

She shoved them back into mine.

"NO! How will you remember me 20 years down the line? If you don't keep them, I will never forgive you," she stated, emphatically.

With that comment, I gave up, holding them lightly in my hands. I didn't want them to wrinkle, so I let them rest in my palms. She seemed delighted by my surrender. A cheery smile stretched across her face. She confidently showed off her pearly white teeth again. She had known from the very beginning that I couldn't say no.

"Thank you, Annalise…"

With her chin pointed high, she said, "It's no problem of mine, Mr. Whittaker."

Just like that, she went in for a kiss on the cheek. Although a light peck, my face flushed with warmth. I could feel my cheeks turn red hot. She probably saw it too, giggling softly.

"Goodbye, Clyde…" She flashed me one last smile.

Her voice lowered. It had the same softness as the way her first words spoken to me sounded. Her eyes had a glaze, which didn't exist before I had told her the news. Her glossed lips were slightly gaped open with a pink tint. She turned around, tucked her hair behind her ear, and walked away, glancing back at me once before disappearing completely as she rounded the corner.

"Clyde!" my father called.

I whipped around. With basket in hand, he scooped me up into his arms. I quickly jammed the mittens into my pocket, knowing that I wouldn't be able to fulfill my promise of putting them in the time capsule. I rubbed the wool between my fingers until felt the roughness of them. A rush of guilt fell over me.

"I told you NOT to leave! How many times are you going to disobey me?" he scolded.

I wasn't given a chance to justify my actions. He shuffled over to the cashier and slammed the basket against the conveyor belt.

"You can't do that in New Jersey. Do you hear me?"

I nodded in response.

"I thought someone snatched you away. You almost gave me a heart attack," he rambled on.

The cashier had a pretty good grasp of the situation, chuckling as my father scolded me. He eventually cooled down, digging in his pockets for his wallet.

"Lemme give you a word of advice, kid. Listen to your parents." The woman slid the bag of chips across the scanner until a loud beep sounded. "I wish I did growing up. Start early so you don't regret nothing, okay?"

"Yes, ma'am," I replied.

After the groceries were scanned, she turned to my father, asking if it was cash or card. My father pulled out a wad of cash and waited until the price popped up on the screen. He gave the lady the exact amount of dollars and coins and tucked the rest into his wallet. She printed the receipt and placed it inside the paper bag. My father grabbed the groceries and held it in his arms as we left the store.

We headed out of the exit. Seemingly, the sky began to brighten from the previous color of gray. Before loading the truck, light footsteps trotted near us. I turned to my left. Madeline charged at full force in my direction, nearly ramming into me. Luckily, she halted a foot away. It was hard for her to speak since she was out of breath from running. She was hunched over, taking rapid, shallow breaths like a madman. I would have offered her something to drink or a chair if I had anything.

She held up a finger, catching her breath. Before I could even ask if she was okay, she struck me right in the shoulder. I clenched the area where she hit me, utterly confused by the attack.

"Ow?" I said.

"You idiot! Were you just going to leave without saying goodbye? What kind of friend are you?" she shouted. "My momma told me after your momma told her. I didn't hear anything from your mouth!"

"Well… surprise?" I scratched my head. "I didn't think you'd care."

"Didn't think I'd care? Do you think I'm that cold hearted? My momma raised me to pity others. Of course, I care!" She threw her arms up in disgust.

"Pity? I don't need your pity." I crossed my arms, feeling insulted and fearing another blow.

"That doesn't matter." She pulled out a piece of paper from her breast pocket. "Here. This is my address. I overheard our mothers talking about how you like to write letters. Send me some while you're in New Jersey, will ya?"

I scrunched my face.

"Why should I? What's in it for me?"

"Well, aren't you my friend? That's what friends do," she defended.

It felt like a pretty strong argument to me, but I wasn't going to let her off that easy.

"Oh yeah? If you were my true friend, answer this!"

"What is it? I can take it," she said rather snobbishly.

"Will you even miss me when I'm down in New Jersey?" I smirked.

"Of course NOT! What kind of dumb question is that? I thought you had more potential, Clyde Whittaker. You really disappoint me," she pouted.

I mumbled a few unpleasant words before turning away.

"That's not how you treat a lady, Clyde." My father ushered me back.

I glared at Madeline, who still stood high and mighty.

"Fine," I snarled. "I have to say goodbye now."

The edge of her lips lifted. I gave her only half a hug, which seemed to content us both. I pulled away and went to load the truck. The groceries were tucked into the back seat with our other belongings. Madeline stayed on the sidewalk as I got into my seat and buckled. As my dad twisted the key, I saw the expression on Madeline's face change. She didn't seem as tough as before. That whole intimidating persona just escaped her at the last second. As the truck pulled out, she waved goodbye. Another familiar person stood nearby. Annalise also waved us away. I leaned at the edge of my seat, pressed up against the window. I fluttered my fingers, smiling as we drove off. I saw *Bleu's Bakery* sweep by us with freshly baked cakes sitting behind the window, then we passed the arcade with the flashing neon lights. *Gracie's Boutique* was next. I saw the nicely dressed worker styling the window mannequin with the latest fad: a polka-dot skater dress with a bow around its waist. I saw a few familiar nameless faces from around town. Since the town wasn't very big, we passed through it pretty quickly. As we pulled away, I caught a glimpse of the last moment of my youthful days in this town. I didn't know when I would return. I took it all in, planning out my blinks so I wouldn't waste a split second of it. With my hand pressed against the window, I waved with my other, saying my final goodbyes to the town and everyone in it, for the next time I would return, Caershie would never be the same.

Chapter Fifteen

New Jersey

THE TRUCK FLEW OVER A LARGE bump in the road, suddenly waking me up from my nap. It was though we never left. It wasn't anything like I imagined it to be because it looked exactly like Caershire. The thundering clouds hovered over us as we came closer to the inner city of Swindon, New Jersey. The towns looked similar to those back at home. There weren't any tall skyscrapers that broke through the clouds. The streets weren't nearly as packed as I thought they would be. There weren't any flashing lights or hectic drivers. The stores were a little worn down but still held business. The streets weren't in their greatest state. Potholes covered almost every inch of the road. There were casual strollers, walking their pets on leashes, and the stop lights held the same amount of time between each color—red, yellow, and green.

The yellow light turned red. We stopped behind the white line. The truck jolted a bit before coming to a complete stop accompanied by sharp screeching. I slipped down in my seat to below the window. The sidewalks were a little closer to the road than in Caershire. The people didn't look too friendly. They took one look at our license plate and snarled with disgust. Yet, my father kept a persistent smile. He bobbed his head to the clearest, non-static radio station, which played something along the lines of some rock band that I couldn't quite keep in memory. The light turned green. My father signaled and took a right turn. We rolled down a smaller road that had very little business along the sides, passing by a mural painted on the side of buildings with a kid drinking Cola. The paint had slowly chipped from the bottle of soda in the hands of the kid. The farther down the wall, a few people in black glided spray paint cans across the wall. At times, the can would choke up and spurt out uneven coats of black paint on the brick wall. The artist shook the cans relentlessly beside their heads, listening to the clanking of, what I assume, a small piece of metal hitting the aluminum as they shook them. They returned to the wall, the paint now spraying flawlessly onto the brick. My father noticed them and sped up.

"You can't be running around in these streets, okay? This isn't Caershire," my father warned me.

It only took one look at this place for me to promise to comply. Caershire was my playground. I wove in and out of those streets with my parents by my side. Most of the inhabitants of the small town knew me in some sort of way. I didn't want to meet these people. They didn't seem like they wanted to meet me either.

We turned another corner into an even smaller street. It was a neighborhood that had pretty decent housing. It wasn't too fancy. The houses had garages and square yards. The yards didn't hold much promise of adventures waiting to happen. It was enough for two lawn chairs and a small round table to put our glasses of lemonade on. A lady in red dashed out of her minivan into her house, protecting her freshly done hair from the drizzling rain. As she dug into her purse for her car keys, she glared at our passing truck. I heard the screeching of tires once more. I lurched forward. My father signaled to turn left into the driveway of a house. The house was colored greyish-blue, making it seemingly average amongst the other greyish-blue houses. The lackluster houses didn't stand out in any sort of way. What made our old house special was that it was the only burnt sienna house that existed in that tiny neighborhood.

As the bumper approached the whites of the garage, he slowly pressed down on the brakes then shifted the gear into park. A bushel of bright flowers sat in pots on the ground. Beside the steps was a bed of dirt with shovels and fertilizer nearby. He opened the door, leaving it slightly cracked. A draft of wind came through it. He grabbed the handle at the bottom of the garage door and lifted it up. It emitted a loud squeaky rattling noise. As he released the handle, the door flung upward, rolling up and down for a bit before settling. He hopped back into the truck, the car door slamming shut, and drove it inside. The lights dimmed. I squirmed in my seat, unfamiliar with my surroundings. The garage smelled of freshly cut birch wood and must. A few spiderwebs made homes to some flies and, of course, spiders, but there weren't enough to classify it as an old house. The truck headlights illuminated the fluttering dust. I popped open the door and unbuckled my seat. My father pulled a string to turn on a single light bulb then shut the garage door. I stepped up on the stairs leading to the garage door entrance to the house, peeking inside the square window. With barely any furniture, it looked plain. I saw the staircase with the shiny white handrails, not rough brown like at home. The kitchen had an opening that was wide and almost connecting to the living room with a short hallway separating it.

I stuck my hands inside my pockets, tugging on the loose threads that wove the pocket to my coat. I looked back at my father. He untied the rope that bound our belongings in the bed of the truck loose. With an echoed *plop*, the heavy rope hit the ground. I turned back around, looking through the square window. Inside, I saw a young boy running down the steps with a cheery smile. An older man came chasing down after him. The young boy had ash brown hair and a few freckles on his nose, similar to mine. He ran around the coffee table, slamming his hands against it once he was trapped by the man. He naively darted to his right and was lifted into the air by the man, soaring in the sky before plopping down onto the couch. They both fell into a fit of laughter, clutching their stomachs for a single breath. The more I stared, I began to see the image clearly. The older gentleman was my father, and the young boy was me.

I smiled.

Sometime during the many years I was going to spend in this house, maybe, just maybe, through the cramping of my wrists from writing constant letters to send back home and through the rejuvenating phone calls I get to have with my mother on how

Caershire was thriving with two less Whittakers in the small town, I felt that things were actually going to be okay.

January 24, 1998

Dear Annalise,

I got to New Jersey. it looks like Caershire. How is it at home? is it still nice over there? it is rainin here. I don't like the streets. people are not nice. You were nice to me tho. I miss playing in the woods. we do not have that here. maybe you could send a picture of two of the town. I miss it and u.

Love, Clyde Whittaker

January 25, 1998

Dear Annalise,

I slept in my new room for the 1st time. Dad said I have to sleep in my room cause I am getting older. I ride the bus to school cause my dad works and cant drop me off and the peaple are mean to me. Well they aren not mean to me but they did not let me play with them on the play ground. 2 boys said I am not aloud to go on the swing. The teacher was nice though.

I am hungry and I will talk to you later. Bye!

Love, Clyde Whittaker

178

January 30, 1998

Dear Annalise,

I called mom from the new house. she said she wants to call me everyday now. Can I call you to?

Love, Clyde Whittaker

180

Febuary 5 1998

Dear Annalise,

Is it snowing in Caershire? Mom said it was snowing again. It snows in New Jersy to. It is pretty here. I miss home still. I hope you stay warm.

                                Love, Clyde

Dear Clyde,

Hey ugly. How is New Jersey? I think its boring. Send me some gifts when you come back. Your mom gave me your address. She told me to tell you she said hi (and that you are stupid). Okay bye

            Not love, Madeline

184

Febuary 7, 1998

Dear Annalise,

Today was my 1st day of school. I do not like it. Some kids think I am weird. Am I weird? I hope u do not think I am weird. How are you today? I am okay. I am still sad I moved. I want to go home. Okay, I will talk to u another day.

Love, Clyde Whittaker

Febuary 14 1998

Dear Annalise,

Happy Valetines Day! Im sorry I cant get you flowers or candy but I wrote you a letter. I hope you still miss me cause I miss you.

Love, Clyde

March 27, 1998

Dear Annalise,

I'm sorry I cant send you letters that much now. I still think about you!

Love, Clyde Whittaker

April 15, 1998

Dear Annalise,

I didnt tell you this and Im sorry but I kept the mittens. I wanted to tell you! But you gave it to me and i couldnt say no... I am really sorry! I can't find them cause my dad said he cleaned out the house and I think he gave it away. Please don't be mad at me. I wanted to say something. Write me back. I know you are mad at me and it is my fault. I will try to find them again. I have not got any letters from you. Are you there? I will see you again I promise

Love, Clyde Whittaker

June 7, 1998

Dear Annalise,

Hey. I did not send a letter to each other in awhile. I know you are mad at me for the mittens and I am sorry again. Dont treat me badly please. I said we will meet again. I will find them for you.

Love, Clyde Whittaker

P.S. Smile ever day for me will ya?

194

Dear Clyde,

Hey, its your bully here. Your handwriting sucks. I cant read anything. Also I asked your mom if I can visit Benjy to give him a gift. I gave him chicken bones. He said he missed you stinky. Come back home.

How is new jersey? Is it boring still? I bet. You dont send enough letters. I will tell you if Benjy says anything. Okay Bye

Not Love, Madeline Bleu

November 30, 1998

Dear Annalise,

Happy Thanksgiving! I am thankful for my friends (you) and my mom and my dad. Thank you for sticking by me. My mom didnt eat with us for the first time. She called us to say grace but she said she had to watch grandma. I was sad but she read me to bed that day. She sent me pictures of her with grandma too. I hope you had a good dinner with your family!

Love, Clyde Whittaker

December 3, 1998

Dear Annalise,

It's my birthday! I am now 9 years old. My dad got me a cake and my mom sang happy birthday to me! You do not have to get me a present but can you write me back? I know you are busy so you don't have to. How is Benji? Is he okay? My friend went to talk to him. ~~They~~ They said they gave him a bone. I think Benji was happy! Did you give him stuff? Its okay if you didn't thats okay. Christmas is coming up soon! I will send you a gift if I can.

Love, Clyde

200

March 14, 1999

Dear Annalise,

Hey, I really miss home. Are you still there? Mom said she has a job and can't call that long anymore. Do you have a phone? No? that's okay.

Clyde

May 20, 1999

Dear Annalise,

I can't send you too many letters because I have tests for my class. It's hard. Wish me luck!

                                              Clyde

204

Dear Clyde,

Goodluck, stupid. Do not fail. I repeat. Do not fail. Or else... I will never write to you again. Okay thats all I wanted to say. Bye

Goodluck said Madline ♡

Dear Clyde,

You aced your tests. You did good. I guess I'll keep writing to you. I bet you aced your test for me, right? Yeah, you did.

You did good, Love Madeline

※ 208

❄ 209

July 4, 2000

Dear Annalise

Happy 4th of July! I hope you are having fun! I know I haven't talked to you in awhile but I hope you are still happy in Caershire, P.A. Keep Benji and my mom happy for me okay?

                                          Love, Clyde Whittaker

210

❋211

September 14, 2001

Dear Annalise,

Are you okay? How is everyone in Caershire? It'll be okay. I promise.

From, Clyde

212

August 5th, 2003

Dear Annalise,

Hey, I bought my first phone. It's pretty cool, too. Here is my number if you get one. Hearing your voice would really cheer me up. I'm not having the greatest of days, but knowing you're on the other side of this letter reading it brightens my day. Keep smiling, Miss Lynn.

Clyde

My number: 845-████

214

Dear Clyde,

I heard you got a new number. Your mom told me.

Here's mine:

(605) 475-6968

Call me or don't

From, Madeline

216

January 15th, 2005

Dear Annalise,

Still no call from you. I really need you right now. Can you call me? Please. School is getting harder, and I need you. I really do. Can you please call me? Or send me a letter back? Are you still there. Please don't leave me, Annalise. I know I haven't been sending you a lot of letters, but I haven't heard back from you. Are you still there? I need you.

Sincerely, Clyde

January 20th, 2006

Hey, mom I wanted to send you a letter for a change. You're probably too busy to send any back and that's okay. Really, it's okay. I just wanted to update you on my life overall. I know we try to call each other almost every single day, but I'm not the most honest person when it comes to speaking over the phone. School is hard. I'm struggling to keep my A's and trust me, I have A's. I guess I just wanted to let you know that Dad is getting more stressed from work. He smokes now. I just wanted to let you know. He smokes a ton. I'm getting a little worried, you know? I miss you mom. I wish I could see you again or you could come see me. I can't keep calling you and looking at pictures. It drives me insane. You're there, yet you're not. It's been a couple weeks since we last called. I know you're working too. Just keep strong for me. For Caershire.

Love, Clyde.

❄ 221

March 28th, 2006

Dear Annalise,

Maybe we should go on a break for a bit. You seem to be busy, and so do I. Can you forgive me this once if I take a break? I promise I'll write you every now and then. Remember me, okay?

Love, Clyde.

August 19th, 2017

Dear Annalise,

It's been awhile, hasn't it? I know we said go on a break, but man, this might have been overkill. How are things in Caershire if you're still there? Is it nice? I hope so. How are you, atleast? I hope you're having an amazing life, Annalise. I really do. You might have made new friends with people who can actually be there with you, but I hope you remember me. You never left my mind for a second. Things have been rough here in New Jersey. We're considering moving back home. My old pops is retiring soon, and he can't work much longer. I stayed with him so he wouldn't be alone, but I feel helpless for my mom. Is she okay? How is she? Did she finish the Giver yet? It's been ages, I know. It's just that she rarely calls now. She used to call every day. Now, it's maybe once a month. Am I getting that old? I can't be. I mean, she called me the other day, but I think the phone was bad. I couldn't hear anything. I guess it's better than nothing. Well, if you see her, tell her to call me soon. Also, I never got a call from you. I guess you just don't want to. That's fine. I understand. Don't worry about it. Just keep in touch. It won't be long until I'm back in Caershire.

Love, Clyde Whittaker.

December 29th, 2017

Merry (Belated) Christmas Mom! You didn't call this year? Why is that? I know I'm getting older, but I haven't forgotten about you. Did you forget about me? I'm kidding. I know you haven't. Just call me when you can, okay? I love you.

Love, Clyde.

226

❇ 227

Dear Clyde and Tom,

Come back home, please.

Claire

228

Chapter Sixteen

Home Sweet Home

My father blew out a puff of smoke, tapping the cigarette outside of the truck window. *Buddump*. The tires flew over an open pothole, causing the watered-down soda to swish in the plastic cup. I fanned the air as the smoke came my way. My father's head turned toward me. He flicked the cigarette butt out the window and cranked it up. The air cleared while the foul smelling tobacco fumes stained the fabric of the seats. I fumbled with my hands, unsure of what to do with them. Neither of us dared touch the radio the entire three hours. We were already lost in our own heads. We couldn't afford another distraction.

A week ago, my mother sent us a letter asking us to *please* come home. It felt like days had passed before the clock ticked to the next hour. I hadn't seen my mother in years. The emotional connection that bound her to the town forbade her to leave. My sickly grandmother, who had just lost her husband at the time, couldn't afford to leave the place that birthed them, nurtured them, and made them into who they were today. Although I hadn't seen my mother in ages, I'd try to call her every single morning and every single night to ensure her wellbeing. Her laughter resonated in the back of my mind. I'd crack a few jokes when I was younger as a nightly comedy skit routine and none ever failed to make her laugh. As the years flew by and I was no longer a young eight-year-old boy, it faded into halfhearted chuckles and sharp exhales accompanied with a short-lived *hmph*. I never quite understood why.

We tailed the red car in front of us. It had a license plate from Pennsylvania, so I knew we were on the right track. My father sped, staring at the road in front of us. As the truck came closer to the bumper of the red car, I nudged my father's arm. We both jerked forward after he suddenly slammed on the brakes, giving way to a few yards between us and the red car. His eyes widened as he gasped for a breath of air. He pulled over onto the grass of someone's property and jammed the gear into park. The emergency lights were switched on.

He covered his face with his heavy hands, pressing his forehead against the top of the steering wheel. I placed my hand upon my chest, holding back my pounding heart. His heaving breaths gave me cause to worry. I gently patted his back, unsure of what to say. My father grew to be a tempered man. I learned to choose my words carefully. I blamed it on the stress from his work. It tired my old man out. He still had a few years before he could retire, and every day that passed by, I felt the weight of his desperation grow stronger. His head stayed down and kept silent until his cell phone suddenly rang. He jolted upward, snatching the phone from the cupholder. It flipped open, answering the call.

"Hello?" he spoke.

I heard the high-pitched words melded together into an incomprehensible sentence. My father nodded every so often.

"Mhm," he mumbled.

I leaned in closer to catch at least one or two clear words to give me some context.

"We're half an hour away. I haven't reached the town yet." He glanced at the clock. "How is she, Shane?"

I slumped into my seat. The conversation was with a caregiver of my mother's while she was apparently bedridden. It's not that I didn't care. I did care. I could even say I cared too much. It was just easier not to hear things. Pretending things never existed became easier than acceptance. I pressed my ear against the door panel, listening to the sounds of cars rolling over the road next to us.

"We'll be there soon."

The call ended. My father dropped the phone back into the cupholder. He covered his face with his hands again and took in a deep breath. I opened my mouth to speak, holding my tongue briefly to think about what I was going to say.

"I can drive…" I suggested.

He took his hands away from his face, peering up at the roof of the truck. He didn't speak a word or acknowledge my suggestion. He kept staring with his concerned eyes, battling with himself about whether to give in. Finally, he unbuckled his seatbelt and opened the car door. I did the same, hopping out and switching places with my father. I buckled myself into the driver's seat, adjusting the mirrors to fit my needs. I had the directions printed on a sheet of paper, which did little to guide me as my memories of the route began to piece together. I waited until the cars passed by before whipping the truck back onto the road. It had slickened from the previous day's sleet and previous night's merciless chill. I stayed below the speed limit, only speeding up when cars appeared behind me. Being in the driver's seat, I felt more in control of my actions. It almost made me want to turn the truck around and head back to New Jersey. Morally, I couldn't do so without seeing my mother first. My heart rate increased with the more distance we covered. My eyes glanced at the gas meter every five minutes in hopes of it suddenly becoming empty. The line stopped at the indication of three-fourths of a tank. I shook my head at the silly attempt to buy more time. As I turned right at the street light, we entered the road that only led to the small town of Caershire, Pennsylvania. I pressed down on the brakes, the red lights illuminating the road behind us. What had once held farmlands and empty fields was now inhabited by ruralistic homes, lined side by side along the road. The trees in each yard were identical. A chill ran down my spine. I feared that my own childhood home would have lost its one-of-a-kind appeal and conform to the cookie-cutter look of the newly built homes. I didn't want to find out.

My father squirmed in his seat. He batted his eyes as we approached the familiar, worn-down sign of *Bleu's Bakery*. I slowed the truck. Madeline's face had faded in color. The sign had ripped, making it look like she had more missing teeth than the original image. The slogan was barely legible. Yellow wasn't the greatest choice of color in the first place. A car honked behind me. I snapped back into focus, speeding up. Soon, we passed a sign that read: YOU ARE NOW ENTERING CAERSHIRE, PENNSYLVANIA. This was my first time seeing this sign. It didn't sit with me right, somehow.

I continued down the road until we were stopped by a red light. The streets were empty with barely anyone walking on the chipped sidewalks. Behind the cracked windows of businesses, the open signs blinked lifelessly with little expectation of seeing customers. *Gracie's Boutique* had a new name. They went by *Milly's Boutique* now. Although it didn't pertain to me at all, the name didn't suit the look. I didn't feel like it belonged to Milly. The light turned green. We crept down the road, taking in the view of the forgotten town. One of the larger grocery store chains had replaced the small one in our town. The arcade remained, but it didn't have the same flare. The neon lights looked dull. They flickered off and on uncontrollably. Of all the businesses that had been burned into my childhood, only one stayed true to its former state. *Bleu's Bakery* displayed its freshly baked goods on small stands in the window. The walls had been repainted. The bright blue hadn't dulled a single shade. Inside, I saw Mrs. Bleu and Mr. Bleu with bright smiles stretched across their faces as they served the only customer sitting alone at a white table.

My father coughed into his sleeve then pointed toward an empty parking lot.

"Go over there. I need to get something from the store," he said.

I signaled right and turned into the empty parking space. We parked in front of a small handy mart. I twisted the key out from the slot and dropped it into my pocket. My father and I got out of the truck, closing the doors behind us.

"I'll be right back. I'm just going to check out the town for a bit and catch up on things," I said.

He nodded, then we parted ways.

I trotted down the sidewalk, careful not to trip over the cracks in the cement. Where salons and banks used to thrive, empty buildings took their place with "for rent" signs posted on the windows. A car, presumably going over the speed limit, sped by, the draft flinging loose newspapers into the air to plaster against the sides of cars and windows. I checked the date on the newspapers, which read a few weeks to a few months ago. I kept walking forward. Although the sun shone brightly, no one came out to soak it in. In fact, I was the only person on the sidewalk at that moment. There used to be plenty of strollers back in my day. I'd ask to pet some of their dogs as they walked by. Sadly, today wasn't the day. As I went by the thrift store, something caught my eye. Hanging on the hooks was a pair of bright yellow mittens. I stopped in my tracks, taking a second glance at the mittens. I ran up to the window, cupping my hands around my eyes to see clearly, then hurried to the entrance. I swung open the door. A draft sent my hair flowing away from my face. The owners greeted me as I entered with bright smiles and welcoming faces. I hastily made my way over to the gloves, hesitant to take them off the rack. I slipped the string, which tied in a loop, off of the hook and rested them in my palms. I flipped them over, finding the white calla lilies stitched near the rim of the mittens. This had to be them. They still felt soft to the touch and smelled like lavender. I rubbed the wool between my thumb and index finger, finding the roughness. It was all there.

I whipped around, accidentally knocking into someone. The clattering of items bouncing off the tiles sounded. Loose pins and game board pieces scattered the floor. I reached down to pick them up along with the person.

"I'm so sorry..." she apologized.

I recognized that voice; although, when it was spoken to me 20 years ago, it wasn't so sweet. I looked up. Through the brunette bangs, I met her chestnut-colored eyes.

"Madeline?" I said, somewhat terrified that I possibly mistook a complete stranger for a childhood friend.

At first, it seemed like she wasn't sure who I was. Her face scrunched with an attitude. Then, her eyes widened.

"Watch where you're going, idiot!" she shouted.

I was taken aback by her sudden remark.

"There's plenty of space in this store. You don't have to go around shoving innocent people," she snarled at me.

I couldn't tell if she was serious or not. In some ways, it sounded like sarcasm, but I could never tell with her. She gathered her belongings and held them in her arms. Her lips pursed, glaring at me. Before I could stand up again, she dropped all her items to the floor and took me in her arms in a welcoming hug.

"You didn't send me a letter or a text to say you were visiting? You really are cruel, Clyde Whittaker," she scolded, separating from the hug. "I thought you would have changed up in New Jersey, but you're just the same coldhearted scrooge as when you left."

"Hold on, wait a minute. I'm the coldhearted scrooge? I'm not the one who sent a letter with a REJECTION hotline number with 'call me' written in it," I refuted. "Frankly, I didn't have much faith in the number anyways."

"Yeah, sure. You were probably sitting in your bed crying all night from the rejection." She rolled her eyes.

"As if I'd cry over your stupid rejection letter." I rolled mine, also. "It's not like I called it five hundred times or anything..."

I awkwardly leaned against the shelf, accidentally knocking over a few knick knacks from above. A squeaky rubber duck that looked particularly like my old duck Marvin bounced off my head and onto the floor. I sharply coughed, attempting to regain my dignity. A few seconds passed by before we made eye contact again, which inevitably caused us to break into gut busting laughter. Her hand held onto my shoulder as she struggled to regain composure. My arm stretched across my waist, clenching my sides. We came together, wrapping our arms around each other once more. This time, it was genuine.

"I'm so glad to see you again, Clyde." She squeezed me tighter. "It's been so long."

"It's nice to see you, too," I said, challenging her strength and squeezing tighter.

The clicking of heels echoed nearby. Hovering over us was the owner lady with her hands on her hips. She didn't have to say anything before we apologetically bowed out heads, gathering the loose items scattered across the floor. I picked the fallen items from the ground and placed them on the rack beside me. We both got up and ambled over to the checkout counter. I safely held the mittens in both hands, careful not to harm them.

"Who are those for?" Madeline took a peek at the mittens. "Lady friend?"

"What? No. These are for my… mom? Yes, these are for my mom," I replied.

Her eyes narrowed. "Okay…"

The owner rang up Madeline's items and displayed the price on the screen, which she paid in exact change. I went up next, handing over the mittens. The owner took one look at them, smirked, then scanned them into the system. The mittens were only 50 cents. I dug out two quarters from my pocket and dropped them into the palm of the lady's hand. I then grabbed the paper bag which held the mittens and rolled it up neatly. We left the store shortly after.

My father sat outside the handy mart, lighting a cigarette. I hated when he smoked.

"So, how's life, Whittaker?" Madeline asked.

I shrugged.

"It's not looking too good right now, but it's nothing to be concerned about." I kicked a pebble with my shoes.

"Oh? How so?"

I chewed on the insides of my cheek. Frankly, I didn't know why either.

"It's just weird being back here. It's been awhile, you know?" I stopped at the bench and motioned for us to sit. "Shall we?"

She glanced at me with her glimmering eyes and sat on the worn-down wooden bench. She crossed her legs with such elegance that I almost lost sight of the old Madeline.

I took my place beside her shortly after.

"I can assure you that not much has changed since you left. It's still the same old Caershire, Pennsylvania," she said.

I shook my head.

"I'm sure *Milly's Boutique* hadn't been here all my life. My mother would throw a fit if it did." I scoffed.

She turned, striking me with her desolate pupils. A plastic bag skidded across the sidewalk as the winds picked up.

"How is she? Your mother…"

"I don't know…" I replied, peering up at the clouds. "She just told us to come home all of a sudden."

My eyes swayed over across the street. Golden locks bounced on the head of a familiar person. Her steps were long, making it seem like she glided across the sidewalk. She wore a bubblegum pink coat with wool on the rims of her sleeves. As she turned, I saw the face of an angel.

"Annalise…" The name escaped my mouth unconsciously.

"Annalise?" Madeline repeated.

I couldn't pull my attention away from her. All the letters I sent led up to this very moment. I couldn't let her slip away now.

"Hold on, give me a second."

I came off the bench and waited until the street was clear before sprinting across to the other side. She didn't notice me. As soon as I stepped on the sidewalk, she walked into the new grocery store. I followed her inside. Somehow, in the array of aisles and large racks of produce, I lost her. I wove in and out of each aisle in desperate need of finding her. I checked in the candy aisle, hoping that she still had a sweet tooth. I checked the cereal aisle, the meat section, and the produce to no avail, so I ended my search. The workers grew suspicious of my actions. A random adult running up and down the aisles didn't register as completely stable. I walked out of the store in defeat. I must have missed her on the way out.

My father waved me down with a cigarette in hand. Madeline had vanished. I lowered my head then made my way back over to the other side of the street. My father dug the butt of the cigarette deep into the ashtray and left it there to die out. I opened the truck door and hopped inside. My father joined me. I slid the key into the ignition and cranked the engine. Before pulling out of the parking space, I turned on the radio and cracked the windows slightly. The tires squeaked as I backed out. I changed the gear to drive and made my way to the route home.

The farther in we got to the backroads, the streets seemed to get lonelier. The backroads were much more peaceful than the rest of the town. It created a nice transition to my home. The clouds parted, allowing a bit of sunlight to fall through. It illuminated the path toward my house. I turned the street and followed the light. The trees were bare with little to no birds resting in them. From the corner of my eye, I spotted my father's plot of land. It caught my father's attention, too. I slowed the truck as we passed by. To our relief, the dogwood tree still thrived strongly among the dead trees. I approached the burnt sienna-colored house. A small candle sat on my windowsill with a promising flame. I took a deep breath in, pulling into the driveway. There were two cars parked near the house. In the garage, a 2000 Honda Accord rested under the canopy, which I recognized as my grandmother's old car. My mother used it after we left Caershire and took the truck. I assumed the other car parked on the road was my mother's caregiver's car.

Once we had pulled into the driveway, I parked the truck and twisted the key out of the ignition. My hand gripped the door handle, not wanting to push it open. I waited until my father made the decision to open his before I opened mine. We slowly got out of the truck, carefully closing the truck door without making too much noise. We shuffled across the walkway, kicking a few pebbles along the way. My father put on a brave face and rang the doorbell. Light footsteps approached the front door before it swung open. Shane, I assumed, stood before us with a concerned look. He had a soft demeanor, which was complemented by his thin frame. The bags under his eyes reflected his sleepless nights. He stepped aside, allowing us to come in. We entered, taking off our shoes.

My nametag, smudged but legible, remained above my cubby. For old times sake, I placed my boots inside it. They wouldn't fit completely, so I had to squish them down a bit. My father didn't bother putting his shoes in his cubby, which still had his name written above it as well. We began climbing the stairs, creeping up each step with Shane leading the way as if we needed him to guide us through the home we forgotten. When I made it to the last step before entering the top floor, my heart sank to my stomach. I had the sudden urge to throw up. My hands trembled as I grabbed onto the railings. It felt rough, unlike the house in New Jersey.

We all stood outside of my parents' room where my mother rested. Shane lightly knocked three times then pushed open the bedroom door. I allowed my father to block my view at first. I heard him hold his breath for a mere second. When I felt ready, I peeked over his shoulder.

My throat clenched up. The feeling in my fingertips numb. This couldn't be my mother. The woman lying in the bed before us was not the same woman who brightened the atmosphere with a single smile, broke the silence with her laughter, and tucked me in bed at night when I couldn't sleep. I saw none of that. All I saw was her sunken face, caving in slightly around her cheekbones. Her body appeared unhealthily thin and darker in complexion. She gasped with every breath. She had lost her luscious golden locks and wore a beanie to hide her frail, thin hair. Her arms looked scrawny and fragile. I wanted to look away, but I could not. I stared in disbelief, wanting it all to be a nightmare I'd wake up from and cry about to my mother and father at three in the morning.

"Mom..." I muttered, my voice slightly cracking.

Her eyes slowly opened. I couldn't tell if she could see me clearly, but I knew she was in pain. Seeing her eyes made me hurt. Yet, when her eyes focused on us, a smile grew across her face. It wasn't the half done smile. No, she showed her teeth with confidence. A tear ran down her cheek. Without holding back, I released mine, too. I had this moment mentally built up from when I had first hopped in the truck and left Pennsylvania, and now, I was finally able to release everything.

Her lips were slightly chapped with a rosy tint to them. She mouthed voiceless words. Frustrated, she tried once more. I saw the glimmer in her eyes as she opened her mouth to speak.

"Hello, Clyde…" she hoarsely whispered.

I took a deep breath in, letting it sink in.

Without a doubt, the woman resting on the bed, weeping to the sight of her husband and son, forcing a smile that pained her to attempt, was truly my mother.

※ 246

Chapter Seventeen

A Mother's Touch

I HELD MY MOTHER'S HAND as softly as I possibly could. Her bones were brittle like an elder's, but she hadn't aged nearly enough to receive that title. I rubbed my thumb against her skin, which had lost its elasticity over time. She told me holding her hand helped her fall asleep. She hadn't gotten much sleep in the past few weeks. Us being there with her helped her feel rejuvenated when she awoke. That was the least I could do for her.

My father entered with a tray table of food for my mother along with her medication. I placed my finger upon my lips to ensure my mother's uninterrupted rest. I pointed over to the radio, signaling for the volume to be turned down. He placed the tray beside the bed and turned the radio knob to a lower volume setting. I continued massaging her hand. Every so often, she'd shift in her sleep. I heard her mumbling a few words, but that was nothing out of the ordinary.

My father crouched down beside me on the floor. He placed his hand upon my shoulder. I looked back at my mother, who still slept soundly. I released her hand and left the room with my father by my side. He promptly shut the door and led me into my old bedroom. When I entered, I could picture the action figures stacked upon my shelf along with the cluttered mess of workbooks and journals on my desk. I imagined seeing my clothes on the ground from the previous day's wear. I also saw the lit candle sitting on the windowsill, but I knew at least that it was real. The feeling wasn't how I had imagined it to be. Moreover, it was a mourning of my innocence rather than bittersweet nostalgia. I was robbed of the emotions I should have felt.

We sat on the bare mattress, our weight sinking into the foam. It had been a week and a half since we'd been here, yet no one had said a word about my mother's situation. I needed the answers I rightfully deserved to hear.

"Why won't you tell me what happened to Mom?" I said, getting straight to the point.

My dad looked at the floor. I was able to see the bags that had formed under his eyes and the scruff of his chin, and I knew that this wasn't just a simple diagnosis that could miraculously be treated.

"I don't know where to start," he said, shaking his head.

"Why is she so weak now? I don't understand. What happened?" I stammered.

He took a deep breath in and swallowed hard. His hands were visibly shaking from the five cups of coffee—all straight black, no sugar or creamer—he had throughout the night.

"Do you know why I bought a house in New Jersey?" he began. "Because your mother loved it there."

As his muscles tensed, I knew he craved a cigarette at this very moment. He wasn't allowed to smoke around the house with my mother's declining health, but also, my mother hated cigarettes. It stained the furniture with a foul smell that every house guest could recognize. He wouldn't have smoked around her even if her health was stable.

"That can't be true. She loved Caershire," I mentioned.

He shook his head, blinking slowly.

"She used to visit New Jersey when she was little and fell in love with it. It was because her parents loved it here in Pennsylvania that she stayed. It was small and comfortable and easy to retire in." He leaned back. "I bought that house because your mother finally decided she wanted to leave—get out of Caershire."

"Why didn't she?"

"Because there was always something that kept her grounded."

He swiped his hands across his jeans and stopped at his knees, clenching them to relieve the pain. His knees worsened with time. It was hard for him to drive, but he insisted when we got the letter. I'd say it was harder for him to accept he was aging than anything else. I wouldn't want to let go of being young either.

"Before we took you in, Claire really wanted a child of her own. She'd cry to me every night on how unfair and cruel life was to us sometimes." He fiddled with his thumbs. "We finally had a chance. We really did. After the day we took you in, we felt so lucky, we tried again. You were the lucky charm in our life."

He clasped his hands together and brought it up above his mouth. Tears began to weld in his eyes. He held his blinking for as long as possible to avoid the eventual stream of tears down his cheeks.

"It was going so well until it wasn't... and his name was going to be Benjamin." He choked up on his words, allowing the tears to fall. "When we told you that you were going to have a younger brother soon, you were so happy, and so heartbroken when we couldn't give you that."

I felt a lump in my throat develop. I tried to swallow as hard as possible to get rid of it, but it wouldn't budge. I couldn't breathe or speak no matter how hard I tried. A part of me wanted to scream for him to stop and that I wasn't ready to hear the ending of the story. The other part of me desperately craved answers.

"For days on end, you cried in your mother's arms," he sobbed. "You wanted a younger brother so bad, and we couldn't give him to you."

He met my gaze with apologetic eyes. They were glossed over with stubborn tears. I had never witnessed someone say *sorry* without annunciating a single word, but he did exactly that, and I was terrified.

"We thought that the plushed animal you called Benji would fix everything, and it *didn't*."

At that very moment, the light at the end of the tunnel dimmed and there was no hope for me to escape.

I shook my head violently.

"I wish I didn't know. I wish you didn't say anything from the start," I erupted. "You gave me a toy and decided that was going to patch things up? I needed a person. I needed you guys. I needed mom. I needed Annalise. I needed someone!"

I shot up out of my seat, clawing at my chest. My hands ran through my tussled hand, yanking at each strand. I gasped for a single breath through my merciless tears.

My father took his hands and swiped down his entire face.

"You know when you gave him the name Benji, it tore your mother apart, but she still went on with it for you. Every single time you mentioned his name, it broke her, piece by piece," he stated with such promise that his actions were all innocent and I was the enemy.

"I was just a kid! I didn't know better. I didn't even know mom had problems having a child of her own until you told me that she wasn't even my real mom!" I screamed.

The burning sensation between the bridge of my nose and my eyes built up. I paced the floor.

"My whole life is probably a lie," I scoffed. "Go ahead and ruin me. Tell me everything I need to hear."

My father's gaze stuck to the ground. He didn't look up. His body stayed motionless as if he was mentally preparing for something. I stood in front of him, awaiting his response.

"Your mother has cancer," the words left his mouth.

My heart sank. The nothingness returned after decades of its absence. My legs had lost all feeling to them by now. Although I had slight suspicious after seeing my mother's state, the last string that tied me to denial was violently severed by the truth.

He opened his mouth to speak in his last attempt at a fatal blow.

"Your mother was diagnosed with stage IV metastatic breast cancer a couple months ago, and she told me—" he looked upward, blinking heavily "—that she didn't want treatment."

I just stared at my father. My entire body began to numb. I thought I was ready, but I wasn't.

"So you knew… you knew, and you didn't tell me?" I clenched my fists. "Every silent call with her in the last few months weren't because she lost service. She was too weak to speak to me, and you knew that… why didn't you tell me?"

He closed his eyes.

"She didn't want you to know…" he revealed. "She didn't want you to get too attached to her if that time came around."

My throat closed up again.

"But why? Why didn't she tell me? If I knew, maybe I could have spent more time with her…" my voice broke into cries. "I just don't understand why…"

I covered my mouth, sobbing into my sleeves. My father immediately got up and wrapped his arms around me, allowing me to rest my head against his shoulder. I relied on him to keep me upright. I couldn't stand on my own two feet anymore.

"Why would she leave me in the dark like this?" I cried.

My father could no longer answer my question. His part was finished, and now all he could do was comfort me.

A ringing sound came from my parents' bedroom. We had given my mother a bell just in case we weren't there when she needed us. Immediately, we ran in, crouching down beside her. You could tell by the look on her face that she had rested well, but as soon as she saw our reddened and tearied eyes, it all went to waste. Her brows furrowed. My heart ached. I hadn't yet wiped away the tears that collected on my lashes. Loose tears streamed down my face. I smiled to assure her that I was okay as so should she be, but I found it difficult to keep my composure. My mother wiped my tears with her thumb. I closed my eyes, using all my strength to keep it all back, but I just couldn't. I broke down, shielding my eyes from hers. Just as I was about to leave the room, she tugged on my sleeve. My mother weakly lifted her hand. I gave her support with mine. She brought it up to my cheek, brushing it lightly, her skin soft as silk. A single touch made my entire body feel warm again. I didn't need her to wrap her arms around me to feel safe. Her touch was just enough.

She smiled back at me.

My heart no longer ached. Everything, through the heavy thunderstorms and hectic day-to-day chaos, felt alright again.

Chapter Eighteen

Sweet Claire

It was an early Sunday morning. The Bleu family came to visit my mother. They were kind enough to bring a few items from their bakery for our family to enjoy during this time of distress. They closed the shop down just for my mother, too. A few of my relatives on both my mother and father's side came to visit from across the state of Pennsylvania. I had never seen them before, but somehow, they knew me.

Madeline tagged along with her parents. She had the right amount of comfort and humor to make the day worth living through. I was grateful that such a person existed.

We sat outside on my porch, swinging our legs back and forth over the ledge. My father asked if I could give my mother some time to catch up with her friends and family. It's selfish of me to say, but I felt like I deserved the most time with her. I held some sort of contempt against every person in that room because every precious second they were in there could have been used with me and my mother.

I fell asleep at her bedside the night before, which I haven't done in ages. My neck cramped from sleeping in such position all night long, but I was actually able to sleep just as soundly as she did.

Madeline's hand intertwined with mine. She leaned her head against my shoulder. We stared off in the direction of where the road cut off at the top of a hill. I closed my eyes, desperately wanting to bring back the memories of my mother and me together when I was younger. She would always scold me for playing outside in the cold. I got sick often as a child because I never listened to her.

The guilt began to eat me up inside. I wanted to go back and make things right, but I couldn't. What I had now was basically it. I would have to live with these feelings forever.

"Do you remember that one day you showed me your hideout area?" Madeline asked.

"Yes, I remember," I replied, still looking straight ahead.

The sun began to set on the horizon, displaying an array of oranges, blues, pinks, and purples. A flock of birds flew over us. They followed their leader, whisping around in a V-formation. I watched as they dived down into the woods where the dogwood tree laid.

"Do you remember leaping over lava pits and climbing trees to escape Bigfoot?" she recalled.

"Yes, I remember."

I suddenly saw flashes of memories with my best friend, Benji, trotting up the road and into our yard. He rolled around in the mud, tugging at the ropes. He only barked when he was with me and no one else, and he didn't make a sound with my parents. There was something about him that connected with me as a kid. I could never let that go, whether or not he was real or a figment of my imagination.

I expected her next question to be somewhat along the lines of losing my best friend, but no.

She simply asked, "Do you remember the Rubik's Cube you gave me?"

I smiled.

"Yes. I remember."

260

Chapter Nineteen

Truth Be Told

My eyelids laid heavy upon my face. I watched as the hospice care workers hauled the stretcher into the black vehicle. They enclosed my mother in a large navy covering to ensure that her corpse would be safe. I lightly placed my hand on the side of the van, silently praying that it would get to the morgue safely. The hospice worker opened his arms wide. I accepted the much needed hug. He patted me on the back and muttered something in my ear, which I failed to catch before he pulled away. It became harder to see as my eyes swelled up.

She couldn't be dead. I continued to deny the facts because I had been so used to anything but the truth. I couldn't handle it anymore.

The black van pulled away, leaving my father and I to mourn the loss of the most innocent soul ever put on this earth. I stood in the driveway, watching the black van until it went past the woods and up over the hill. I watched until I could no longer see it anymore.

"There's family and friends coming to visit. We should get the house ready..." my father said.

He slipped inside the house, keeping a strong face as others were coming over soon. I looked ahead at the hill and wished to myself that maybe the van would come back and she'd be alive. I waited outside in the freezing cold for some miracle to happen. I rocked on my heels, fumbling with the thoughts inside my head. I paced the driveway, hoping to find something to distract myself with, but there was nothing. I walked over to the garage and rummaged through the hoarded junk. I flipped over wooden boards and pieces of firewood but to no avail. In anger, I pulled back my leg and kicked the items as hard as I could, sending a shovel to slide off the racks and into the grass. I went over to pick it up, feeling guilty for kicking it in the first place. Finally, it struck a chord in me.

I threw the shovel on my shoulder and took off toward my father's land. I wasn't as light as I had been as a child, my footsteps pummeling the pavement beneath me. Each step became heavier and heavier. I clutched my chest as my lungs began to burn, but I couldn't stop. I cut through the grass and into the maze of trees. The dogwood tree stood out amongst them all. I trudged forward until the sight of the obvious mounded area of the time capsule became clear. I hunched over the tree, completely out of breath. I wasn't ready to see what was inside, but I wanted to know. I needed to know.

I slammed the blade into the dirt and tore off the top layer, tossing it over my shoulder. I jammed the shovel blade in deeper, using my boot to stomp it down farther, then scooped out another layer. The reddish-brown mud transformed into a warm hickory brown color. In the next go at cutting through the earth, the shovel went in with a *thumph*. I paused for a second, taking in what I just heard. I carved around the object, creating a much bigger hole than necessary. Finally, I stuck the blade under the object then pushed down on the shaft. As the other end lifted, the ripped roots stuck out from the dirt. I carefully dropped the box on a flat surface and crouched down near it. I could see bits of the grocery store bag through the dirt. I dusted it off with my hands, catching tiny rocks underneath my fingernails. I didn't want to disturb the contents inside, carefully peeled off the grocery bags until the sheen of blue velvet shone through. It still had the smell of fresh cedar wood. I held it in both hands, mesmerized by how it hadn't aged like the rest of us. I stood up, walked over to the tree, and placed my heels against the base. *One, two, three.* I put one foot in front of the other. *Four, five, six.* I made my way to 27 steps.

In the area where I stood, Benji awaited my return. I got down on my knees and stared at the dirt ground. Flakes of white began falling from above, landing on the velvet before dissolving completely. I looked upward. A few snowflakes landed on my lashes and my nose. I tightly shut my eyes, letting the iciness nip at my skin.

"Is that the time capsule?"

I opened my eyes. A curious Annalise stood before me. Her face seemed ageless. Every wrinkle that could have occured during the last 20 years was replaced by a seamless stretch of porcelain. Her cheeks remained the same shade of pink—a slightly less saturated rose color—all these years. Tiny white snowflakes rested on her lengthy lashes. I looked down at my hands. They, too, had lost all signs of aging. My winter coat felt two times bigger with the name *TOM* embroidered on the pocket in yellow thread. Around us, the snow had collected into large white dunes. It became piles by the second.

"Where were you?" I asked, slightly choking upon my words. "Where were you when I needed you the most?"

Her glistening gaze stole my breath away. The blizzard ceased, turning to specks of dust fluttering in the air. The trees and snow dunes muffled all sounds that could have occured. Her mouth curved into a smile. She remained silent. I had waited two decades to hear her voice again. I wanted an explanation—a reason why she had abandoned me. I wanted to embrace her in my arms again and play amongst the bare trees. I wanted to speak to Benji like I used to do. I wanted to go to Doggy Heaven. I wanted so many things, but she didn't give me anything.

"Is it because of the mittens? I got them back- I mean I think they're yours—No—I *know* they are yours." I reached into my pocket and pulled out two bright yellow mittens.

Another strong breeze swept by before her rosy lips moved apart.

"Did you miss me?" she giggled.

Twenty torturous years to hear her voice, and she tittered at my longing, my suffering.

"Did I miss you? You can't even imagine how much I missed you, Annalise." I shuffled forward. "I ached so much for you. I really need you now. Out of any other day, today is the day I need you the most."

I was so close to her. She really hadn't aged. There was no wrinkle in sight.

"I love you, Annalise. I really do…" I admitted, shamefully.

Her smile faded. She took a step back.

"No, you don't."

My heart sank. The feeling was like no other.

"I don't love you?" I queried. "I spent years sending you letters and wondering where you were. If that's not love, what is it?"

"Desperation." Her eyes became teary. "I gave you comfort, and you mistook it for love."

Her words pierced my heart like an arrow. I clenched my chest, carefully replaying her words in my head to assure what I was hearing was correct.

"You don't mean that…" I stepped closer, my shoe sinking deep into the snow. "Please, tell me you don't mean that."

I cautiously reached for her hands, which she then allowed me to hold.

"Do you remember when you told me that- that you'd be there whenever I was upset? I-I sent you so many letters, and I got none back from you," I stumbled over my words. "How come you ignored me when I returned? You disappeared all of a sudden. What's up with that?"

She stared at me with solemn eyes. They were hollow and unforgiving.

"I kept my promise." She remained calm. "You don't need me."

"Yes, I do…" Tears ran down my face. "I need you…"

I collapsed into her arms, resting my head on her shoulders. She didn't shove me away nor mock my sorrow. No words were said. Her hands ran up my back. Although my thick coat separated her skin from mine, I knew her tender hands were warm. I squeezed her tighter, desperately wanting her to return the hug.

"You said you hated change, right?" she said. "Why is that?"

I rested my head on her shoulders, my eyes wandering down to a bundle of Calla Lily budding in the snow. I didn't want to answer the question. If I did, she would leave me without a second thought.

"It's safer, isn't it? Or at least it feels safer…" she continued.

The snowflakes danced in the air before landing onto a single Calla Lily leaf. It had no chance of survival, melting almost instantly into a tiny droplet of water.

"When you shield the scary things out, it just makes you fear more." She moved her hand down my back. "You're just scared, Clyde…"

In an instant, the soft petals bloomed through the dewy green encasing. The deep cerise hues bled through the white. Behind the matured flowers, a lone bud failed to bloom. I saw the bright yellow peep through the charetruese of the leaves, longing to be fully grown like the rest of them.

"You can't keep hiding in the dark, Clyde." She gave way for some space between us. "You have nothing to be scared of, okay? The world isn't as cruel as you think it is. I promise"

I sniffled, swiping my sleeve across my eyes.

"What will I do without you…?" I muttered.

"There are already people in your life who can do the same things I do. You just have to let them." Her brows furrowed. "This is the last time I'll be seeing you, and I want you to promise that you won't miss me. If you miss me, then everything we built between us has no meaning."

She held up her pinky.

I shook my head, rejecting her invitation to promise.

"Either you promise me or I'll never forgive you, Clyde Whittaker, and I know that's your greatest fear," she sternly said. "I will only mention your name in vain rather than appraisal. Do you want that?"

I pursed my lips, shaking my head, no.

Our pinkies intertwined, securing the promise. My arm became heavier for a second, dropping by my sides.

She puffed her chest, wiping away the rolling teardrop with a relieving smile.

"I promise you that you'll be fine. It'll hurt a little bit, but you can handle it. I know you can." She backed away. "This is our goodbye, Clyde Whittaker."

I saw the timid Calla Lily bud bloom before my eyes, sprouting petals of gold. The snow around it melted in an instant, being soaked up the earth.

I closed my eyes, nodding regretfully.

The feeling of remorse lingered around me. I peered down at the dandelion-colored mittens. Before she turned away, I grabbed her bare hand and placed them in her palm. Her dainty fingers curled around the mittens as her dimples found their way on her rosy cheeks.

"Goodbye, Annalise A. Lynn. I hope you'll remember me," I said, forcing a smile.

In return, she flashed her pearly white teeth. It was the last smile I was going to see from her. As she turned to walk away, the snow dunes began to melt as did the snow on the ground. The strong breezes turned to slight drafts. Before the blizzard calmed, Annalise faded into the flurry of snow, and everything finally returned back to normal.

A heavy force knocked into me, latching their arms around my waist and suffocatingly holding me tight. Madeline had her eyes shut all the way as she squeezed me.

I chuckled, returning the hug and lifting her off the ground.

"Your family is worried sick. Are you this stupid to run off again? How many times are you going to do this?" she scolded me.

I grinned, taking my coat off and wrapping it around her. We embraced for another minute or two, soaking up each other's company. The winter's merciless temperatures gave us an excuse to stick together. I stuck the velvet box under my arm and pulled her close as we made our way out of the woods and through the opening of the arch. Hand in hand, we entered the real world again, stepping on the asphalt. I could see the cars lined up around my house. People waited for our arrival.

We made our way down, jogging quickly. The velvet boxed rattled as we skipped. My father stood on the porch, squinting as we approached the house. I brightly beamed, assuring him that we were safe. In return, a smile grew on his face, smoothing every wrinkle on his cheek and creating new ones near his eyes. I jogged down the driveway and up the steps into his arms. As we pulled away, I revealed the velvet box. It didn't process with him at first. Then, as it clicked in his mind, he stared at it in disbelief.

Madeline, my father, and I sat on the wooden floorboards of the porch and placed the box before us. I took a glance at my father to which he nodded in approval. I carefully lifted the latch and took a deep breath in. All the very important aspects of my childhood remained within this box. As soon as I lifted the lid, every secret, every memory, every emotion would pour out. Though this very moment wasn't how I imagined it to be 20 years ago, I couldn't be any happier.

Chapter Twenty

Everlasting Years

I HELD THE HAND OF MADELINE as the pictures of my mother was broadcasted on a projector beside the casket. Her smiles captivated every single person that attended the ceremony. My mother wore her favorite lavender dress from *Gracie's Boutique*. She had on red lipstick, the shade of ripe strawberries, and a slightly pink blush. Her hair had been washed and styled until it resembled that of a hollywood movie star. Her lashes were painted black and made longer. Though, I thought her natural beauty could beat any look of cosmetics. Her favorite purse was tucked in beside her. My father wanted her to be buried with the items she loved the most. I wanted nothing more than for her to be happy.

There were those who cried and those who didn't. We all dressed in black, awaiting the moment when she would be slowly let down into her grave. When close family members were given the chance to speak, I could barely let out a word. It was tougher than I thought. My biggest regret was not reciting a speech upon her resting body, but I couldn't speak. As I approached her casket, I kissed a letter that I had written that contained everything I wanted to say to her but couldn't. It contained what I wished could have happened but didn't. I put it all in a single letter. I tucked it inside her purse and grasped the edge of the beautiful baby blue coffin.

I stepped aside to allow others a chance to speak to her. They had more words prepared than I did. Guilt ate me up inside, but I remembered that I spoke to her almost every night, thousands of miles laid between us.

I grasped the hand of Madeline, pulling her close to me. My father took my other, biting his lower lip as she was lowered into the ground. I couldn't help myself from holding back the tears, but I knew these weren't for mourning. My mother wouldn't have wanted me to.

I tightened my grip on Madeline's hand, glancing over to her then over to my father. After all my years of running away, hiding, and lying to myself, I finally saw the true meaning of content. The timid sun broke through the deterrent clouds to show its respects to my mother. The last snowflake fell upon a single blade of grass and melted away with my final tears of goodbye, signaling the arrival of a bright new beginning.

        The long awaited season of spring.

January 15, 2018

Dear Annalise,

It's been twenty years since I last saw the "real" you. I don't feel the same now. I don't have much to say. I thought I'd have a whole book prepared for you, but in all honesty, I have nothing. I spent the majority of my life wanting to feel like I was something to someone when in reality, I was just chasing a ghost. I guessed I can start by saying thank you. Thank you for being there when I lost Benji. Whether or not he was real, you were there. Thank you for making me feel like I meant something to someone. Or at least, I thought I did. You promised me you'd always be there for me, but you weren't. It's been twenty years Annalise, and throughout those twenty years, I made friends that I'm confident would never leave me. You remember that girl in the arcade? Her name is Madeline. I lied about not knowing her. We met up with each other after I returned from New Jersey. She used to write letters to me while I was in New Jersey. I'd send you back some letters too, but I never got any in return. That's okay. I ended up finding every single letter I sent you stashed in the attic of my house. I don't know if you just forgot about them or you didn't bother to check the mailbox, but they were there. Every single one of them. I'll give you the benefit of the doubt. Madeline wouldn't even give me back the letters I sent her. She said she was going to frame them. Can you believe that? She's crazy. Anyways, I just wanted to say goodbye. Formally. When I last saw you, I was a mess. I had tears in my eyes and snot in my nose. It wasn't the prettiest sights to see. I'm sorry you had to put up with it. I really thought you were the girl of my dreams. I was so naive back then, and I hope you understand.

Please don't forget about me. I know I'm not allowed to think about you anymore. Since I have to grow myself, I can't keep thinking about you. That doesn't mean you can't keep me in your memories. You seem to be doing well since I left Caershire back in the 90's.

Anyways, I just wanted to give you a final update. We're not sure what we're doing with the two houses and the land. It's heavy work for my old pops to take care of. It might come down to us selling something. The question of which is still in the air. A part of me wants to move on from this house and from Caershire. Another part of me wanted to preserve the memories. Until we decide, we'll be in Caershire for a bit. And every night, I'll light the candle by my windowsill for when you need to find me again. I want you to remember us for me. I can't keep you circling in my head any longer, so I grant you access to keep our memories alive. Do what you want with them, but never abandoned them.

Lastly, I wanted to say thank you again for being there for me when we were kids. Because of you, I now know what it means to be content with myself. I can stand on my own two feet. Of course, I have close family and friends, but I'm able to go on with my day without you. That's probably the cruelest words I have ever written, but I know that it holds bittersweetness between the both of us. Again, thank you, Annalise. I bid you a final farewell, Miss Lynn.

Sincerely and Lovingly,
Clyde Whittaker

❋ 279

Author's Note

To all my friends and family, thank you for supporting me every step of the way. It was a long, tough journey, but I couldn't have done without the support of my peers. I highly anticipated this moment since the first word was typed onto the page, and it wouldn't have been possible without everybody's generosity. I want to thank my parents and my friends for believing in me, my editor and mentor for guiding me, and my english teachers for pushing me towards my highest potential. I truly appreciate every single person in my life. Thank you all for making this possible.

Made in the USA
Middletown, DE
27 January 2020